We Will Always Be Together

WE WILL ALWAYS BE TOGETHER

Margaret Seiders-Metz

iUniverse, Inc.
New York Lincoln Shanghai

We Will Always Be Together

Copyright © 2006 by Margaret Seiders-Metz

All rights reserved. No part of this book may be used or reproduced by any means, graphic, electronic, or mechanical, including photocopying, recording, taping or by any information storage retrieval system without the written permission of the publisher except in the case of brief quotations embodied in critical articles and reviews.

iUniverse books may be ordered through booksellers or by contacting:

iUniverse
2021 Pine Lake Road, Suite 100
Lincoln, NE 68512
www.iuniverse.com
1-800-Authors (1-800-288-4677)

ISBN-13: 978-0-595-37948-4 (pbk)
ISBN-13: 978-0-595-82317-8 (ebk)
ISBN-10: 0-595-37948-6 (pbk)
ISBN-10: 0-595-82317-3 (ebk)

Printed in the United States of America

DEDICATION

This is dedicated to all those that have lost their loving spouses or are taking care of their loved ones who have incurable diseases. It's not an easy job but someone has to do it. And who is better qualified then a spouse who can be gentle and understanding because of the love each has shared to one another. May God Bless All Of You!

Acknowledgment

Thanks to the staff at Burbank Prairie Trails Public Library who helped me gather information to use with my own opinions and thoughts for my book. A special thank you to Bob Metz, the Martinez, Schmitt and Seiders families who were there for me when I needed them.

CHAPTER 1

GROWING UP

As a small child growing up, time was never important to me. I had no need for an alarm clock to wake me up. I woke up when I was well rested. I played till I got tired. I ate when I was hungry and when I grew sleepy, I slept. When I started school then a clock was needed so that I got up in time for school. I had a certain amount of time to get home for a hot lunch, then rush back to school.

As I grew older I had less time to play since more time was needed for homework and my chores to do at home. After supper was finished I would help my mother clear off the table and do the dishes. When all my work was finished I watched some black and white television with my parents until 10:00 PM which was bedtime, so off to say my prayers and fall asleep till the next day.

Saturdays we scrubbed the floors on our hands and knees, and cleaned the house up real good. After all my chores were done I was allowed to go out and play. Sundays started off with going to Mass with my parents. On the way home my dad would buy a newspaper and I would get to read the funnies. Sometimes we would go to visit my relatives or they came over to see us. Occasionally we would partake in a movie or shop on Maxwell Street where my mom found some great bargains. We always took streetcars since mom or dad never drove and if they did we couldn't afford a car anyway.

It was fun until you had so much to carry that your hands ached. Mom would take my sisters Eva and Rosemarie too. Then the four of us would stop off for lunch and bring home some pastries for my dad. We weren't rich or poor, I guess you would call us middle class. My dad was a good provider and my mom never had a bill collector wrap on our door. She was a good manager of money.

My clothes were mostly hand me downs from my sister Eve but were always clean and in good condition. My mom sewed the holes so good you could never tell where it was ripped. I attended St. Mary of Perpetual Help Grammar School and am now attending their Catholic High School. My parents couldn't afford to pay for my tuition so I cleaned up the classroom after school to make up for the costs.

I would clean the blackboard and dust the erasers, sweep the floor, water the plants, empty the waste paper baskets and dust the tables and shelves and window sills.

When I was in my junior year, my father took very ill and no money was coming in to pay the bills, so I quit going to school and got a job. I took anything I could to make money. I was a bagger at Hillmans, and a sales clerk but it didn't pay enough. So I went to work at Spiegels. It was a better paying job and the money sure helped pay those bills.

My parents received a letter from the School Board saying that I had to go to school until I was sixteen, it was the law. So I quit my job so my parents wouldn't be fined and went to Princeton High School but not for long. It was so dangerous that one day the teacher locked us in our classroom to keep us safe. It sure was very scarey. Some of the kids were crying and afraid to leave the room.

There were teenagers looking for trouble and started throwing empty soda and beer bottles at some of us kids. When they finally went away from the school grounds the teacher let us out to go back home. Even the teachers were afraid of the kids. When I got home and told my parents what had happened, they refused to let me go back to that school.

They received another letter stating they would be fined if I did not attend school since it was the law until I was of age. So I went to a vocational school which was very far to travel from home. I would leave my house at 6:00AM and return home at 8:00PM. I had to wait on dark corners in bad neighborhoods for my transfer of buses.

Again my father refused to send me back to school. He told the school board that when you get those rotten kids off the streets and make it safe for my daughter to attend school, then I will send her back to school. I stayed home for three months until I reached the legal age where I was free from the school board threatening my parents and me.

I was now legal age to work so I went back to Spiegels and was hired back without any hassel. I worked sometimes seven days a week. Ten hours a day during holidays. The money was good and I liked the job and the people I worked with. I seemed to get along with everyone. That's where I met my best girlfriend Dolores Niedzwiecki. We became friends from the first time we met. We had a lot in common except I loved dogs and she was terrified of them.

We were the same age and both of us were Polish and Catholic. Neither one of us drove, we always took the bus or on nice days we walked to work and back.

I handed over my whole paycheck to my mom and in return she gave me bus and lunch money. I seldom took the bus and would walk on nice days, it was only seven blocks away. Mom always had a hot meal waiting for me when I got home from work. My dad recovered and went back to work, at Armour & Company after eight months recovering from his illness. I continued to work instead of going back to school.

I didn't have time for fun but once in awhile I did go dancing with my best friend Dolores Niedzwiecki. She would loan me one of her pretty dresses to wear since I didn't have any of my own. After I turned eighteen I met this handsome guy at the dancehall. We seemed to hit it off and danced every dance together.

He had hazel eyes and was around 6' tall with a good built. It was love at first sight for both of us. My parents were very nice to him and liked him a lot. His name was Robert but I called him Bob. He was very polite and had good manners. He was gentle and yet very strong and a hard worker.

After dating Bob for nine months he asked me to be his wife and I said yes. We had a small wedding at St. Albert The Great Catholic Church. We knew of many couples that had a big wedding and they just ended up in a divorce. Bob and I wanted our marriage to last forever. Big weddings are just to show off. The money we saved by not having a big wedding went for a deposit on our new house.

It was like a marriage made in heaven, we were so happy and in love. After ten months of marriage I gave birth to Maryann, our new little angel from heaven. God was mighty good to us. Now we were a complete family with a house, a car, a dog and our newest addition Maryann. We were living on cloud number nine.

The following year we were blessed again with another angel, a little boy named Mark. The babies were adorable. I was constantly washing diapers or sterilizing bottles for their formula. There were times I made their formula with one eye open, I was so tired. They were a handful but it was all worth it because I loved them both. I took care of my husband and raised our children as I was raised.

When my husband woke up, a hot breakfast was waiting for him on the table and his lunch was packed with a full thermos of fresh hot coffee. I always kissed him good-by and the babies slobbered over him before he left for work. We stood by the door and waved good-by as he pulled out of the driveway. When he returned home after a hard days work we greeted him with a kiss. The house was always clean and a good meal prepared.

He would play with the children, read the newspaper, and mail before we all sat down to eat as a family. After the meal was finished I would wash the dishes and he would wipe as we talked to each other. When the children were finally sleeping we had time for each other. We never went to bed angry. We always kissed goodnight and the children said their prayers early in age with our help from habit.

Our babies were never left alone or neglected. They were fed, changed, played with, rocked, sang to and got plenty of fresh air since I took them on daily strolls.

Even in the cold weather, I would just bundle them up warmly and off we would go. We all got plenty of fresh air and exercise from walking a lot. We went shopping or visited with my relatives or friends. When anyone came over to our house, they would comment on how clean my house was that one could eat off the floor.

That's how my mom raised me. She said to always keep your house clean because you never know when someone might drop in on you. My mom taught me plenty, how to cook, bake, sew, manage money, to be a good wife and mother and to have God in your daily life. There was always homemade cake for my company.

I was so close to my children that I could tell when they weren't feeling well. Sometimes all they needed was a little love while other times I had to take them to see our doctor. I use to do all my housework and laundry while my children slept. Noise never brothered them. They loved to have me read to them and also watch cartoons.

My children never smelled from a pissed up diaper or puke like some babies did. Neither one of them ever had a diaper rash since I kept them dry and clean. They were great company for each other. When one would giggle the other followed and when one cried so did the other. Sitting inbetween them made you feel like they were bookends on each side of you.

They were like my play dolls except these cried and wet and moved their arms, legs and head. As they got older they would get into everything especially my pots and pans or covers. They would play more with them then their own toys. I would give them my big mixing spoon and they would beat on the utensils like a drum. The more noise it made the more they laughed.

You don't have to spend a lot of money on toys, kids have so much fun with things you have in your house. Any thing that is shinny or makes noise. They would even play with the clothespins. We play games with Cheerios and then enjoy eating them too. They learned to share their toys. The only problem I had was when they both wanted to be held at the same time. It's hard to console them both at the same time when you only have two hands.

When they started teething they were so crabby and overtired that the only solution was to take them for a ride in the car where they would finally fall asleep. We took them everywhere. Picnics, amusement parks, playgrounds, vacations, visiting, shopping, long walks and car rides, even to church.

I love rocking them to sleep on my shoulder with their little arms around my neck. They look like little angels when they are sleeping and every once in awhile they will smile or giggle out loud. A few times they even cried in their sleep. Oh what I wouldn't do to sleep like a baby.

Mark and Maryann are growing so fast. It seems like yesterday they were my little babies and now both of them are in kindergarten. They are having a lot of fun playing and learning and making friends. I hang their pictures that they make in school on the fridge, although sometimes I can't tell what it is. They told me once it was a picture of daddy and me well I'm glad they told us because we never would of guessed what it was.

Our house was like Grand Central Station with all their friends over all the time. We should hire a crossing guard or install a stop light for all the traffic coming and going. Our only problem is that there is only one bathroom and it sure gets a workout. I don't mind all the kids, this way I know where mine are, and with whom. I usually supply them all with cookies, kool ade, ice cream or snacks to nibble on while they play. Even Queenie has fun chasing them through the house.

The girls play dress up with some of my old dresses and shoes, jewelry and they use my curtains for veils when they play bride. Or they pull out all the Barbie dolls and clothes to change from dresses to gowns or bathing suits or short sets. The boys on the other hand play war or spaceman or trade baseball, basketball or football cards.

Sometimes they would all play school together, but everyone fights to be the teacher, so I step in and tell them to take turns. Our poor dog even gets dressed up and wheeled in a buggy. She loves it especially when they eat their snacks at their tea parties. Queenie gets a cup and saucer too. I've joined them for some of the tea parties but it is very hard to sit on those little chairs.

When it is real hot outside then they all jump into the pool in the back yard and have a ball splashing each other. Oh, to be young again. Bob and I would join in to play Monopoly, Go Fish, War, Old Maid, Bunco, No Peek, Candyland or if it was nice outside we just went to the park on the swings and slides and to play in the sand.

It was fun to watch them play Hide and Seek because Queenie would give them away wherever they were hiding. The neighbors kids liked coming to our house and it showed since they were here during school vacation at 9:00 AM and left at 3:30 and even stayed for lunch. Saturdays and Sundays were our special days to spend with the family or we would visit our relatives.

Bob's parents and mine are deceased but we have a lot of friends and relatives that have children close to our kids ages to play with. The kids have other pets besides Queenie, our watchdog. Bob built a cage for the rabbit outside. Maryann has a Guinea pig in a cage in her bedroom, and Mark has six fish in a tank in his bedroom. Everyone wants pets but you know who gets stuck cleaning up after them.

We had a turtle and a frog but somehow they got away and we couldn't find them anywhere. The fish get replaced when one dies. I don't think the Guinea pig likes me since everytime I pick her up to clean her cage she poops and wets all over me. I put her in a big plastic ball and Queenie chases her all through the house. This way they both get their exercise.

The children were playing carnival and used a blanket to make a tent. I heard this big crash and there was my long glass top from the cocktail table in pieces on the floor. Of course no one knew how it broke. As children do, one blamed the other. Oh well at least no one got hurt, after all accidents do happen. A glass can be replaced but a child can't. They were sorry and apologized. I never did find out how it really broke, and probably never will.

As a Catholic I made sure that our children were baptized Catholic when they were born. And they both made their Holy Communion and Confirmation. They attended Mass on Sundays and Holy days with Bob and me. They believe in God and say their prayers every night. They go to confession and receive Holy Communion every week. Both of them have graduated from Dulles Grammar School and are now attending Reavis High School.

Mark is a freshman and Maryann is a sophmore. They both are doing good with their grades but Mark could do a little better if he tried more. They both come home for a hot lunch and we get to spend time talking to each other. After school I have cookies and milk or hot chocolate waiting for them or a sandwich to hold them off until supper time. They go to the corner to wait for their dad to come home from work and when they see him coming they race him home unless it's raining out or to cold.

When it snows we all shovel and build a hugh snowman on the front lawn and end up in a snowball fight. I threw a snowball at Bob and it landed in his mouth. I laughed so hard I nearly wet my pants. But Bob got even with me when he washed my face in the snow. We try to do everything together like a family, but there are somethings that I refuse to partake in like horseback riding. I'm terrified of horses, so I sit in the car when they go. They all can swim pretty good but not me,. I can't even float. I was held under water by a boy when I was fifteen and almost drowned. So ever since then I will walk in water up to my hips and that's as far as I go. And please don't dunk me or throw water in my face because I get panic stricken.

The kids go roller skating and ice skating but I have a bad leg so I sit and drink hot chocolate or stay at home. They dance and that I love to do especially the polkas and jitterbug. I love to dance fast or slow. Our vacations are usually in Wisconsin where we do a lot of fishing, relax and meet many people that are very nice and friendly. Mark and Maryann enjoy fishing, swimming, riding horses and making new friends. They end up with kids their own age and play cards, pool or just walk and talk around a bonfire toasting hot dogs or marshmellows.

The adults sit around the bonfire too. Only our talks are about the fish the men caught or the big one that got away. And the women talk about receipes and kids. Everyone was friendly and very pleasant. Sometimes they would fry the fish they caught and pass it around with hush puppies and beer to wash it down, of course the kids had pop.

Even Queenie our dog had a ball chasing squirrels and going on the boat with us. We had so much fun that no one wanted to go home but our vacation time was over and Bob had to go back to work or he wouldn't have a job. It's funny how time can fly so fast when your having fun.

The long trip home wasn't to bad since we all join in playing guessing games of things in the car starting with a certain letter and color like example, I'm thinking of something silver, black and green and starts with the letter R. Mark guessed it right away. I guess he caught me looking at it. It was the radio so now that he guessed it right, it was his turn. When we got tired of playing, we sang songs together or ate snacks. It helped pass the time and sometimes they fell asleep. I always kept awake talking to Bob and pouring him coffee.

We all got out to stretch out legs and visit the restrooms when Bob stopped for gas. I would take Queenie for a potty call and a short walk so she could stretch her legs too. We made a stop in Madison Wisconsin to eat and buy some fresh cheese. They had this hugh statue of a cow. I had Bob, Maryann and Mark pose under the cow with their hands up to look like they were holding the cow up and snapped the picture. I got one of Maryann standing next to a statue of a lumber-jack that looked almost real.We told everyone it was a picture of her boyfriend and it made her blush. I even got some nice pictures of Queenie with a frog that scared the crap out of her when it jumped.

There were so many pictures of the beautiful scenery in Wisconsin and of the fish that we caught plus some of the kids with their new friends they met. I still had more to take before the roll was finished.

Inside there was this big Moose head hanging on the wall and Bob posed under it with his finger up the Moose's nose. I hate to tell you which finger it was. I like to take silly pictures so that when you look at them it makes you laugh and to remember the good times you had on that vacation all together. Laughter is your best medicine. We are a very happy family and even laugh at our own mistakes.

If you lose your sense of humor your lost and sad. I remember a day when Bob just got through winding up the garden hose and walked into the house, well one look at him and I split a gut laughing. He was wearing sunglasses but one of the colored lenses was missing and it looked so funny. I guess you had to be there and see it for yourself to really see how funny it looked.

I hurt my knee real bad and it never healed properly so I can't run, jump, squat, skate or dance the polkas or jitterbug anymore. After getting out of the car I decided to throw a snowball at Bob and my aim was perfect as I hit him in the head. I tried to run fast so he couldn't catch me. My legs were going two fourty but I wasn't moving at all because I was on ice. Well no need to tell you what happened, yep, I got it, my face washed in the snow again. I must have the cleanest face in the world. Even though we are getting older we act like little kids. Could we be going through our second childhood? If we are, we sure are having fun doing it Acting silly keeps us young and happy.

They say your only young once, so I guess we still haven't grown up. Life is to short so enjoy it. Serious people get ulcers and I don't intend to ever get them, although I may give them to people. I love life and every thing about it, and intend to enjoy it to it's fullest. I'm not a perfect mother, I've made mistakes with my kids. Like the time I had to rush Mark to the hospital with a bad nose bleed that wouldn't stop. When we were walking down the hospital hall, and Mark's head was tilted back with a cloth filled with ice over the bridge of his nose, a doctor stopped me and asked me if I was trying to kill my son?

He told me Mark could have choked on his own blood with his head back like that and showed me the right way. To keep his head straight and put pressure on the bridge of the nose. I tried that but it still didn't stop. The doctor finally stuffed gauze in each nostril and continued putting pressure on the bridge of Mark's nose until it finally stopped bleeding.

Never a dull moment with kids, right. Bob and I never left our kids home by themselves. We either took them with us or got a reliable sitter, and always left our number where they could reach us in case of a emergency. You never know when an accident can happen. So far we have been lucky because we never received that frightening call, when they tell you. I'm sorry but your child is dead or in the hospital.

The first time we went out without the children, we felt very guilty leaving them home with a sitter. But then parents have to have some enjoyment by ourselves. And now that they are older and go out by themselves, they don't feel guilty about leaving us home by ourselves.

I'm just thankful that they tell us who they are going out with and where they will be in case we have to call them for an emergency.

Maryann graduated with high honors and the following year Mark graduated by the skin of his teeth. Between you and me I think the school just graduated him so they didn't get stuck with him for another year. Mark's grades were okay but he was the class clown and never took anything serious. But now that he is older, he does have a good head on his shoulders.

Mark has followed in his dad's footsteps and became an electrician. Maryann on the other hand is working in the hospital with children who have cancer. Bob and I are very proud of both of them. We must of done something right bringing them up. They are always polite to everyone they meet and try to help out whenever they can. We all still meet at St. Albert The Great Church on Saturday's for mass and then share our dinner together afterwards.

They both work long hours and save every penny they can, that goes into their bank accounts. Each has their own car that they paid for with their own money and the auto insurance too. How many kids do you know did that? Most parents buy their kids everything but then how do you expect them to learn responsibility? My kids knew money didn't grow on trees. They took better care of their cars since they paid for them with their own money.

We raised our children right, teaching them how to pay for things by themselves. And if they couldn't afford to pay for it, well then it meant you shouldn't buy it. They have learned to save their money by depositing it in their bank accounts that I started for them when they were born.

Every penny they received for their birth, when they were Baptized made their Holy Communion, Graduations, Birthdays, Christmas, Easter, Confirmation, Thanksgiving, Valentines Day, Halloween and any extra money they received went into their accounts from odd jobs they did for neighbors.

When they were of age to buy their cars, I handed them their bank books. They were surprised to see how much money they saved in all those years. After purchasing their cars, auto insurance, sticker, plates and whatever else they needed, they still had money left in the accounts. And they were so proud that they paid for it all with their own money.

I tried to teach them the same way my mom taught me. Never to borrow because it's twice as hard to pay back. Think twice about cosigning for a friend since if they don't pay the bill you are also responsible for the payment. Both learned how to cook, sew, bake, wash and iron clothes, make a bed, keep a house clean, shop for sales and to save money in the bank.

GROWING UP   11

I'm proud and so is Bob that Maryann and Mark will be able to handle things on their own. They even knew what to look for in a mate when your ready for marriage if that's what they planned to do. My children won't have to be dependent on anyone of course we are always here to help them if they need it.

But one never knows if they will be around to help after all no one lives forever. They are good kids and I know they will manage fine on their own.

CHAPTER 2

▼

MOVING OUT

Mark came home from work all excited because he found a cute apartment close to his job and was thinking of moving in it if we didn't mind him leaving us. Bob and I agreed that it would be great for him to experience living on his own. We told him if it didn't work out he could always move back home. We all pitched in to help Mark move and get settled in. It was a nice apartment.

Mark still came over for some meals and we all went to mass on Saturdays as usual. Mark wasn't alone for to long. He fell head over heels in love with Amber and before you knew it, they got married. Amber fit into the family as soon as we met her. She was a bit shy and sweet and was perfect for Mark. They had a lot in common and did everything together.

All the gifts they received at the shower sure came in handy for them, starting as husband and wife. Maryann on the other hand had no interest in marriage. Oh, she dated but when a guy got serious, she dumped him like a hot potatoe. She loved kids and when I asked her if she wanted to settle down and have kids of her own, she told me it just didn't fit into her schedule right now.

There is no rush on love. With her hours at work, it was hard to find a man that wanted to date you in the early morning hours. She was content to just take it day by day and see what happens.

Maryann told me she hasn't met Mr. Right yet but when she did I would be the second one to know since she would be the first. She laughed as she waved good-by from her car. Many of my friends told me it was wrong to wait on my family so much. They said I was spoiling it for the rest of the women and I was a goodie two shoes.

I tried to explain that when you love someone, you do everything you can for them. I'm doing it because I want to and not because I have to. That is the difference. The house was so quiet with Mark gone and Maryann seldom home with her long hours at work. It felt just like when we were newly weds, only the two of us and of course Queenie.

I kept myself busy trying out new receipes on Bob. Some you could brag about and others we won't even discuss them. Bob always ate a hot good breakfast before going to work. I packed him a healthy lunch which he took with him after he kissed me good-by, heading for work. When the dishes were washed, I then spent an hour exercising with my pal Richard Simmons and an hour on my exercise bike.

Time for a hot shower which I needed badly. I got dressed in my sweats and took Queenie for a long walk. Then I washed a load of clothes and did my normal housework. Outside to my flower and vegetable gardens to weed and water. I would wash the windows but it looked like rain. Instead I got in my car and did some grocery shopping.

I stopped off to get a haircut which was badly needed. By the time I got back home it was time to prepare supper for the two of us. A couple of times Maryann or Mark and Amber would join us. I didn't mind because there was always enough to go around. I always cook more then what we ate. I'm use to cooking for four people.

Not having the kids around was almost like being on a second honeymoon. Bob would pay so much attention to me that I was getting spoiled but enjoying every minute of it. Everytime we passed one another he would kiss me or pat me on the butt or wink at me. It made me feel like a young teenager in love. He would bring me candy or even a package of gum wrapped in a piece of paper that read "Love Yah" or "My Honey Bun" or For My Sweetums". We would watch some television with the lights off and our arms would be around each other.

When bedtime came, we cuddled so close it was like one person in bed not two. Even sitting next to him in the car, we were so close that it looked like one person in the drivers seat. Our marriage was like a marriage made in heaven. We both were so happy and so much in love. I never had to worry about him leaving me for another woman of course, I never stopped him at admiring other women. He loved only me and I couldn't love anyone else but him.

We both married for better or worst and so far I have only seen the better and it just keeps getting better. I don't think I could live without him and wouldn't want to. If one of us died the other would follow in death soon after. The phone rang and it was Maryann, asking if she could come for dinner that she wanted to talk to us. I prepared three ham slices, baked sweet potatoes, corn, salad and cranberry sauce with coffee and I made some Brownies that she loved.

Bob and I figured maybe Maryann found a guy and was planning marriage, and wanted to ask her dad to walk her down the aisle to give her away. But boy were we wrong! She had no intention of ever getting married since most of her friends who were married, are now divorced or having an affair.

The reason she wanted to talk to us was that she found a nice condo near the hospital where she worked and had a girlfriend who would split the costs of everything. I came right out and asked her if this friend was her lover? But she laughed and said no way, she was straight. Just because I'm not getting married doesn't make me gay. You both don't have to worry, I like men not women!

My friend Jenny and I would just like to try living on our own and we would save transportation money with it being so close to the hospital where we both work. They had nothing to lose, if it didn't work out they would lease the condo and move back home. But they both felt that they could pull it off with no problem moneywise.

So we both gave her our blessing and hoped for the best. After we all finished our meal I packed Maryann a doggie bag to take to work with her. It was nice to see her again. With her crazy hours, we are asleep when she comes home and she is sleeping or gone when were up. I hope things will work out for her, she deserves it being a good kid and hard worker with never a complaint.

She doesn't have much time for fun only work, work and more work. But she loves it so who am I to complain. Someday she will find Mr. Right and raise a family of her own when the time is right. Of course she isn't getting any younger. It's in God's hands what is meant to be.

I'm not complaining but I miss the noise, fracas and cooking for four people instead of two. Believe it or not I even miss picking up after them. Bob said he could help me out in that department and he would start leaving his clothes laying all around. Ha, ha! very funny I told him. At least Queenie isn't leaving us but then she is getting up there in age like the rest of us.

We helped Maryann move her belongings to her new Condo. It was quite nice and had a pretty view of the swimming pool that they could use in the summer. It had a nice little kitchen, three bedrooms, one for her, one for her friend Jenny and the third was to be used for a computer room. There was a nice size living room and a garage for their cars and storage space. With all of us helping out the girls were all settled in and ready to go. It was late so Bob and I kissed them and left.

The next day was a busy day for me. I spent almost the whole day baking and cooking meals for Maryann and Jenny to just heat and eat. I made **Chili**, Chop Suey, Beef Stew, Cabbage Rolls, Lasagna and Chicken Soup. I baked them German Apple Cake and Chocolate Chip Cookies and made a Pineapple Upside Down Cake for Bob, his favorite. I had time so I ran the food over to their Condo. I set everything in a big box. They both were so pleased since neither one had much time to cook with their crazy hours. They had just made a pot of coffee so we sat and had some cake with the coffee and talked awhile.

On the way home I stopped off by Mark and Amber to drop off some baked items and to ask them to come over Saturday night to celebrate Bob's birthday. Amber looked like she was putting on weight although I wouldn't tell her so, no woman likes to hear that. I didn't stay to long but did tell them about Maryann's Condo. They said Maryann called them and invited them to come over tomorrow.

I asked them to please do me a favor and ask them to come over Saturday for dad's birthday. I forgot to ask them when I was there. I hope they can make it. Tell them I'm getting Pizza too, so don't eat. Try to make it by 6:00.

When Saturday arrived Bob was relaxing in the recliner watching television and the doorbell rang. I asked him to answer it because I was busy. He was surprised to see Mark and his wife Amber, and in the driveway Maryann and Jenny were just getting out of their car. It was nice being all together again. Mark told us Amber was expecting our first grandchild. What a beautiful birthday surprise. We both were so tickled, we kissed them both and gave them our congratulations. The Pizza arrived and we all sat down to enjoy it. I lit the fifty seven candles on the cake and we all sang Happy Birthday to Bob. He made a wish and blew out all the candles before the smoke alarm went off. While I cut the cake and added ice cream on each dish, Bob opened all his gifts and cards, and then thanked everyone.

We talked about everything from soup to nuts as we finished our cake and ice cream. The men went downstairs to play pool and talk shop while us women stayed upstairs talking about babies. We asked Amber if she wanted a boy or girl? How she was feeling? When was the baby due? Did they have names picked out yet? Amber didn't care if it was a boy or girl just so it was healthy. She was experiencing morning sickness but sometimes crackers seem to help. The baby was due around September 12th and they haven't yet decided on a name.

It was getting late and Amber felt tired so she called Mark to get ready to leave since tomorrow was a workday. Bob got their coats and Maryann and Jenny were leaving also. We kissed everyone good-by and waved as they pulled out of the driveway. Bob didn't look good to me and I asked him if he felt alright. He said he was okay just tired from a busy day at work.

He took a shower and retired to bed. I cleaned up the mess in the kitchen and gave Queenie a tiny piece of birthday cake after all she was family too. I let her out for the night and brushed my teeth. Then slipped into my silk pajamas and let her back in and locked the doors. Turned off the lights and got into bed where Bob was already sleeping. I leaned over and kissed him good-night like we always did. Then I cuddled close to him and put my arm around him. He was so nice and warm and smelled. oh, so good. I whispered Happy Birthday Sweetie, I love you and fell asleep in his arms.

Bob had a very restless sleep and tossed back and forth most of the night. When we got up the next morning, his coloring was very pale and I asked him if he felt okay. He said he was just very tired that he didn't get a good nights sleep. I thought maybe he was coming down with the flu since it was going around at work. I suggested he see our doctor and he agreed to. So when 9:00 rolled around I called to make an appointment for him and was in luck since someone cancelled theirs. I talked Bob into staying home from work and going back to bed.

I called his boss and told him Bob wouldn't be in today and wasn't sure about tomorrow that it depended on what the doctor said. I did my normal cleaning quietly so I wouldn't disturb his sleep and would check in on him every once in awhile without waking him up. He was sleeping like a baby but his breathing sounded funny. When Bob got up he had a cup of homemade chicken soup with crackers and a cup of coffee with a slice of hot apple pie that I just took out of the oven.

After he finished eating he went in the bathroom to shave, shower, brush his teeth and get ready for the doctors appointment. He put on a pair of jeans with a sweatshirt and his socks and shoes. We left for the doctors office and arrived with time to spare. There were just two people ahead of us so we grabbed a magazine and sat down until they called his name.

We followed the nurse to the doctors examination room where she weighed Bob and then took his blood pressure. She wrote it all down on his chart and said the doctor would be in shortly. After waiting around five minutes the doctor walked in and questioned Bob about his symptoms. He suggested Bob get a blood test and a Cardiogram now. He listened to his heart, checked his eyes and ears and felt his ankles.

After drawing blood from Bob's arm he said he wanted Bob to get further testing done at the hospital to be on the safe side. He didn't like the pale color on Bob's face and the swelling of his ankles also his heart was out of rhythm. The nurse handed Bob orders for his tests at the hospital while I set up another appointment for Bob to see the doctor next week.

From there we went straight to the hospital to get the tests done and over with. After registering at the hospital, they sent us up to the Cardiology floor. There they took Bob in for an Echo Cardiogram and a stress test. He didn't mind the test but he didn't like the IV that was kept in his arm for the Cat Scan with and without infusion.

Bob hated needles but then who doesn't. After he was finished we returned home. Queenie was acting very strange and wouldn't leave Bob's side for a minute. She followed him everywhere even in the bathroom. Bob acted ancy and decided that we all go for a walk. So I got Queenie on her leash and we took a two mile walk. Bob held my hand like he always did. He had a nice strong grip but yet was very gentle. His hands were always so warm. It was nice walking this way. Even Queenie looked forward to these walks with us.

MOVING OUT 19

Bob wasn't to hungry when we got home so we just split a tuna sandwich and a can of diet-caffein free Pepsi. The rest of the day we just sat around talking and watching a little television. Mark called after work to see how his dad made out at the doctor's. I told him we wouldn't know anything until the results come back from his tests at the hospital. He wanted to talk to Bob so I handed the phone to Bob and went to let Queenie outside.

When I returned to the living room I had two dishes of frozen yogurt and handed one to Bob. After he finished, he let Queenie lick the dish clean. I washed the dishes and we both retired to bed. The whole week seemed to drag. And Friday finally came and we left early to see the doctor and find out Bob's results. There was only one woman ahead of him. So we just took a seat and waited until they called us.

The nurse called Bob's name and showed us to the examining room and in a few minutes the doctor came in. He shook hands and asked how Bob felt. He opened the folder and told Bob it's just what I expected but I wanted to be sure. Your heart is damaged and has to be repaired, You have a Coronary Occlusion, which is a total closure of the Coronary Artery. It might be fatty deposits piled up high enough to jam the flow channel or it can be a blood clot plugging up the vessel or heart damage in the heart muscle. I want to put you in the hospital with your consent now.

I want to be honest with you, with the surgery you have a 50-50 chance but without the surgery you won't even survive. Tears rolled down my cheeks as Bob agreed to have the surgery with a sad look. We got Bob checked into the hospital right away and the doctor had him scheduled for one more important test before the surgery. A Cardiac Catheterization. The nurse took us up to his room and got him into a hospital gown and in bed.

She took his vitals and asked him a lot of questions, even asked if he was in any pain right now. A Cardiologist came in and explained the test that he was going to perform on Bob. They would insert a thin plastic tube or catheter into his leg vein. The tube is carefully advanced through the vein until it reaches the heart chambers to find out information about the defect.

I could tell Bob was afraid but he had no choice really. We both felt it had to be done. They came an hour later to take him for the test and the nurse suggested I could go home and come back later because it will take awhile. So I kissed Bob and told him I'll be back later that I was going to let Queenie out. I wished I could of stayed with him and hold on to his hand because I knew how frightened he was.

Bob was always healthy, never even had a headache just hangovers but that doesn't count. When I got home I let Queenie out and sat by the table and cried my eyes out.

Why was this happening to him? He was a heavy smoker years back but hasn't had a cigarette for over fifteen years. He did drink beer but not whiskey. I cooked healthy meals with no fat, no salt, no sugar and look at the results, is it worth it? I started to pray on my rosary to God that everything would turn out alright.

I heated a cup of morning coffee in the microwave and put some peanut butter on a toasted bagel. When I finished I washed out the cup and plate. I called the kids but neither of them were home so I just left a message on their machines. I told them I would call back later with more news about their dad.

I went back to the hospital and found Bob sleeping soundly. I didn't want to wake him so I just sat there and waited till he woke up. A nurse walked in and pulled back his covers to check if he was still bleeding where the doctor inserted the tube. It must have stopped because she took away the ice pack that was lying on the spot. Bob still looked very pale and worn out. I know he was glad this test was over with.

Bob opened his eyes and was surprised to see me sitting there. How long have you been here, he asked? I gave him a kiss and answered, only a few minutes. A nurse brought in a tray with food for him to eat. He said he was starving but I noticed he really didn't eat that much.

I could tell he was still worried like the rest of us. Our doctor walked in with the Cardiologist, Dr. Bump and neither one of them looked happy. Dr. Bump took hold of Bob's hand and said Bob you have a massive injury to your heart muscle. A very large area is out of commission, I'm sorry to say. I'm really surprised that you never had any kind of trouble before this. Especially with your type of job, up and down ladders and carrying heavy equipment all day.

You are existing on only half of your heart. The other half is so damaged it cannot be repaired except with a heart transplant I asked our doctor what caused the damage? He said Bob could of gotten it when he was in service or maybe he was even born with it, they didn't know.

I asked how come no doctor ever spotted it before? They said it was probably because Bob was never that sick or had any kind of problems like now. What happens now I asked? Well the doctor answered we will keep Bob here for a few days to monitor him and place him on medication. After that he can go home but no strenuous work and just wait until we call you, that we have a donor with a heart for him. He told us he wished he had better news for us and told Bob not to worry, wished him luck and left.

I stayed a little while longer trying to comfort Bob. He looked so worn out and tired. I tried to tell him not to worry that everything would turn out alright. Let's just take it day by day and keep our faith in God. I kissed him and left so he could get some sleep. When I got home I called Maryann and didn't lie, but told her what the doctor told us that her dad would need a heart transplant. But we would have to wait until they found a donor.

She started to cry and I wish I could of comfort her to help soften the blow. I told her to pray that her dad would be okay as soon as they found a heart donor real soon. I told her they would keep Bob in the hospital a few days to put him on medication and monitor him then he could come home till they would get a donor with a heart.

I then called Mark and he couldn't believe it and insisted that they got the report mixed up with some other patient. But I told him it was dad's report, just pray for him to get a donor soon and then everything will be okay. The next morning I got up early and went to mass and also received communion and afterwards told the priest about Bob's condition and he said the congregation would pray for him at all the masses.

When I got home I called the hospital and talked to Bob. He seemed in a better mood then he was when I left him yesterday. He said he ate a good breakfast but not as good as mine. Bob said he was so hungry that he almost ate the tray too. It felt good to hear him joking around again. I told him I would see him soon. He said Mark and Amber talked to him for awhile and the chaplain came in to give him communion and they talked and he said he would keep me in his prayers, just keep the faith in God.

I told him if I don't get off this phone I'll never get to see him so we both said I love you and hung up. I stopped off at Walmart to buy more pajamas for him, magazines, hard candies, gum and the newspaper. I found a funny get well card that would make him laugh. It was a picture of a nurse looking at a guy's butt hanging out from the hospital gown, saying I know I've seen you before, I never forget a butt! I signed it, your better half and Queenie, Hugs and Kisses.

When I went back to the hospital Mark and Amber were just leaving Bob's room. They couldn't stay to long since Amber was pregnant, it was to uncomfortable to sit to long. I gave Bob a kiss and handed him five get well cards that came in the mail. As he opened them I went for some fresh ice water for his pitcher. I helped him into his new pajamas and stuck the gum and candies in the drawer.

I laid the newspaper and magazines on his table so he would be able to reach them after I left. Maryann walked in with a vase of beautiful flowers for him.

They sure brightened up the room and smelled a lot better then the medicine smell in his room. She didn't stay to long since she was on her way to work but promised to drop by later again. She kissed us and told Bob to enjoy the flowers and left .One look at her and I could tell she was getting teary eyed seeing her dad this way.

It was like walking on glass around Bob. We wanted to crack jokes to make him laugh and yet we were afraid that with his heart being in such bad condition it might put a strain on his heart from him laughing to much. We talked about how big Amber was getting and Bob said are you sure she isn't carrying a baby elephant since she was hugh? Either she is going to have a big baby or else it's fat.

A couple of Bob's friends Jim, Lester, Okie and Dave dropped in to see him. They told him the guys at work really miss him and that he should hurry and get well. They handed him a card with all the workers signatures and a hugh planter with live plants mixed with silk flowers. Bob's eyes got teary. They didn't want to tire Bob out so they didn't stay to long. The nurse came in with his dinner and it looked good but tasted awful since he couldn't use salt

The doctor came in while I was there and told Bob, he could go home since there was nothing they could do for him here until they got a heart from a donor to transplant into him. He would have to wear a halter monitor and take his medication. He wanted to see him in his office to check that everything was okay in a week. He handed me a diet for Bob to follow and that he should just take it easy and not to overdue anything.

He asked Bob when he would like to check out and Bob answered, yesterday, and we all laughed. The doctor went to sign Bob's release papers at the front desk by the nurse's station. He came back and said your all set now behave yourself or you'll be back in here sooner than you think. The nurse will give you your prescriptions and instructions and will wheel you out in a wheelchair. I'll see you next week in my office unless you have problems call sooner.

I helped Bob get dressed and packed his belongings and we waited until the nurse came in with the wheelchair. It seemed like it took forever for her to come. She handed me papers with his diet, exercises he could do, prescriptions and asked Bob to sign papers. Bob sat in the wheelchair holding the big planter while I carried his belongings and the vase of flowers. Down the hall, into the elevator, out the door and into the car and away we went towards home sweet home. I asked how he felt and he said better now that I'm coming home.

I handed him some cards that came in the mail. They were get well cards from Bob, Ted, Phil, Jim and Norm from the Pavillion.

Queenie was so glad to see Bob and wouldn't leave him alone, she followed him wherever he went. Queenie kept licking his hands until I stopped her before he wouldn't have any skin left on his hands. Bob got comfortable in his favorite recliner and I put a pillow in back of him and covered him with a blanket.

I went into the kitchen and prepared a lite lunch for him. A egg sandwich made from egg whites only and some jello with a cup of apple juice and hot water with a tea bag. While Bob ate I put away his belongings in his dresser and some clothes went in the wash. God it felt so good to have him home with me again.

I called Mark and then Maryann to let them know Bob was home so they wouldn't make a trip to the hospital for nothing. They both were glad their dad was home but was worried that maybe he should of stayed in the hospital in case something went wrong. I told them that both doctors said there was nothing more they could do for him until they received a heart from a donor.

Your dad has to wear a halter monitor at all times and take his medicines on time, he has a diet to follow and some lite exercises to do. They asked if it was alright to come and see him? I asked Bob if he would like some company and he said, you betcha! Mark and Maryann would drop over tonight but wouldn't stay long because they didn't want to tire Bob out.

I fed Queenie and then let her outside. Bob fell asleep in the recliner so I decided to clean up the house while I had a chance. He looked so peaceful. I just sat there for awhile admiring him. He sure looked thinner and was still pale looking. His eyes flew open, I was caught in the act. Bob said come here I want to talk to you.

I leaned over towards him and he kissed me and said I love you. Get me some food woman, I'm hungry! I made him a grilled cheese sandwich on toast with a cup of chicken soup and some tea. I gave Bob his medication with a glass of water as the front doorbell rang. It was Mark with Amber who had trouble walking from all the extra weight she was carrying.

They both kissed me and then went and kissed Bob. Amber teased Bob that if he was still at the hospital, she was going to sneak him out under her maternity smock. Bob laughed saying you have got to be kidding, there isn't any room under there for me.

Just then Maryann walked in and kissed everyone then sat down by her dad. Mark and Amber started to leave because they didn't want to tire Bob out. You could see tears rolling down Maryann's cheeks as she excused herself and went into the bathroom to freshen up. Maryann takes after me being emotional and sentimental. We cry very easily over sad movies, romantic movies even weddings and certain songs.

Bob use to kid us that we would cry if Mickey Mouse and Minnie Mouse broke up and you know what, we probably would. He often teased me that one day I would drown in my own tears. I just can't help it. There is no way to control tears from coming, believe me I've tried everything. Swallowing, chewing gum, thinking happy thoughts, looking over at the crucifix hanging in our church when they play the Ave Maria or Come Follow Me, but nothing works. The tears come rolling down my cheeks.

Everything worked out great today. The kids came to welcome their dad home and stayed awhile but didn't tire Bob out. I'm glad they all decided to drop over, it made a great day for Bob to see them. I'll bet he sleeps like a log tonight.

During the night I noticed Bob was very restless and I asked him what was the matter. He said that he had pain in his chest. I dialed 911 and while we were waiting for the ambulance to arrive I called our doctor to let him know Bob was on his way to the hospital. The medics carried Bob out on a stretcher and I followed. They took him right into emergency while I filled out the usual forms.

I called Mark first and told him dad was back at the hospital in emergency and I didn't know anything else. When I called Maryann, she started crying. I told her not to worry he was with the doctors now and maybe it was only heartburn, but deep down I was scared too. I wish someone would let me know what's going on in there. All things were going through my mind. Finally our doctor came out to talk to me.

He said Bob had a Aneurysm, at the aorta and needs surgical measures to correct this problem or it can rupture. We need your permission to operate right now. I signed the papers and the doctor said he would let me know how Bob was doing that he was in good hands. Maryann arrived and sat next to me while I filled her in about her dad. She held my hand so tight it felt like she was cutting off my circulation.

Mark came in and sat over by us. I explained that Bob was in the operating room now, to repair the Aneurysm before it ruptures. We were all worried since his heart was in bad shape to begin with. Was it strong enough for this surgery? We all walked over to the chapel to pray for Bob.

We sat there praying like we never prayed before. I told Mark to go home and be with Amber now that I would call him when I heard something but he insisted on staying. Mark was pacing the floor, worried with grief as Maryann and me still sat praying for Bob to survive this surgery. I don't know how long we were sitting here but it seemed like days. Our doctor finally came in to talk to us. He said it's over and Bob did great and is in recovery. They removed the Aneurysm and got it in time before it ruptured.

MOVING OUT   25

The ballooning section of the artery developed a saclike appendage which was tied off and removed and the small opening between the blood vessel and the sac was sewn closed. I still wish we could find a donor with a heart soon. The doctor said we could see Bob but only for five minutes and we should go home to rest and let Bob get plenty of rest too. Bob was still out like a light so we didn't disturb him, just kissed him and left.

We all went our seperate ways and I stopped off at our church and went in to thank God for helping Bob through the surgery and praying that now He can find us a donor soon. I went home and let Queenie out. She could sense that something wasn't right. I gave her fresh water and filled her bowl with dog food. I didn't know if I wanted to eat or just go to sleep. I sat on the couch in the living room with Queenie at my side and fell fast asleep. The first and last thing on my mind was my darling husband. I wished I could of changed places with him. I hated to see him in pain although he tried to hide it.

I felt someone licking my face and opened my eyes to see it was light outside and Queenie probably had to go outside for a potty call. So I got up and let her out while I put on a pot of coffee and threw two slices of bread in the toaster. I dialed the hospital and talked to the head nurse to find out how my husband was doing. She said he was doped up so he could sleep good and was still sleeping. I told her when he wakes up to tell him I called and would see him later.

I sat in the living room thinking out loud that the doctors work on Bob's heart but God works on his fate. God is the best healer anywhere. It was so quiet in the house that I could hear my heart beating out loud. I was so worried about Bob getting a heart in time that it felt as if my heart swelled with such great pressure that it could just explode. I silently prayed on my rosary.

I called Amber to see how she was feeling. All she wanted to do was have this delivery soon. She had trouble sitting and standing and was very uncomfortable and as big as a house. I felt so sorry for her. Amber was a tiny woman and not used to carrying all that extra weight. It looked like she gained around sixty pounds. Even her legs swelled. She was having bad pains in her back and I told her to be careful since that's how I went into labor with Mark and suggested maybe she should call her doctor.

I straightened up the house and got dressed to go see Bob. I took a couple of pairs of his pajamas, his toothbrush and toothpaste, deodorant, a comb and a razor with blades. I threw some hard candies for him to suck on. After getting at the hospital I stopped down at the gift store and bought a hugh balloon in a heart shape that read, "My Heart Trobs For You To Get Well." I ran into our doctor and asked him how Bob was doing. He said Bob is not out of danger yet.

His heart is still in bad condition. I wish I had better news for you but until we get that heart he's in God's hands. Just don't give up and keep on praying. He was being paged so I thanked him and he left. As I walked into Bob's room, the television was playing but Bob wasn't watching it, he was miles away. He was so pale and had tubes running every where on him. And his monitor was beeping. Hi honey! I leaned over and kissed him and held onto his hand never wanting to let go. Queenie says arf, arf which means hi dad. He smiled but I could tell he was in pain.

I could feel the tears rolling down my cheeks and tried to hide them from him but I wasn't fast enough as he wiped them with his hand. Everything is okay, you don't have to cry. I told him his heart was the one that suffered damage, but my heart felt like it was on fire and it was shattered into a million pieces when they took you in for surgery. I love you so much and don't want to lose you ever. I couldn't live without you, your a part of me. Promise me we will always be together.

Honey promise me that you will never leave me. I don't know what I would do without you. I need you in my life. Bob said remember when we got married it was for better or worst, well this is the worst, and it will get better. We will always be together honey, I love you and only you. We kissed and a nurse came in to check his vitals. His pulse was running fast and Bob told the nurse that's because my gorgeous wife is here next to me. Another nurse came in with medication for him to take.

You could tell he was hurting but would never complain. The phone rang and it was Amber so I handed the phone over to Bob. While he talked to her I got him a fresh pitcher of ice water. She didn't talk to long, she didn't want to tire him out just to wish him well. I sat talking to Bob and he would doze off now and then, so I just sat there holding his hand and stroking his hair off his forehead. God he was such a handsome guy and I was so lucky to have him. We were so happy together and were good for each other.

Mark walked in just as I was shaving Bob, he looked a little better with all that peach fuzz off his face. Mark commented that Bob didn't have to get all prettied up just for him. Bob told him you'll have to leave if you make me laugh and just looking at you makes me laugh. We all laughed and I told them both to cut it out you know that the doctor said don't over due it. So behave yourselves, both of you. Unless you prefer to stay in the hospital. Bob said I'll behave, honest.

Just then Maryann walked in with a bouquet of flowers. The nurse commented on how pretty they smelled and brightened up the room. I figured as long as the kids were here I would go home and let them enjoy the time with their dad. I kissed them all good-by. Queenie was anxiously waiting by the door to greet me. She sure is a good dog. Even with all this going on she has never had an accident in the house.

I made myself a tuna sandwich and poured a cup of coffee heated in the microwave and grabbed some cookies, put it all on a dish and went into the living room with Queenie at my side and sat on the couch. I turned on the television but couldn't get involved in watching it. I shared some of my sandwich with Queenie which she enjoyed. I went downstairs to wash a load of clothes. When I came up I decided to call Bob.

Hi, sweetie, how you doing? Did the kids leave yet? I'm fine, just a little sore, it only hurts when I laugh so don't make me laugh. The kids left around twenty minutes ago. I told him somebody wants to talk to you and put the phone by Queenie and got her to bark in it. That was your buddie Queenie saying hurry home I miss you. Bob wanted to know how I got her to do that. I said for me she will do anything, you should see her sing and dance, ha,ha. I love you, I won't keep you I just wanted to say goodnight and that I'll see you tomorrow and leave the nurses alone. You will need all the energy you have to get well. I miss you.But you'll be home soon and we can finish where we left off. Love yah sweetie.

It was to early to retire so I took a shower and put on my pajamas. I sat in the dark in the living room saying my rosary so that they would find a heart donor real soon. I must of fallen asleep because when I woke up the next morning I still had the rosary in my hand. I ached all over from the way I slept all hunched over on the couch. I got dressed, combed my hair and put on some makeup and perfume. I went over the mail and wrote out some checks to pay some bills.

I didn't have to make the bed since I didn't sleep in it. I folded the clothes from the dryer, dusted and shook out the runners. I let Queenie out while I filled her bowls with water and food. Grabbed a glass of orange juice and told Queenie, see you later, watch the house and left. The nurse was just changing Bob's bandage as I walked in. She took his vitals and told him she would be back in an hour to get him out of bed for a short walk.

After she left Bob complained that he wanted to check out and come home. I said you can't until the doctor says you can, but he insisted he wanted to go home. I could tell by his monitor he was getting upset so I just told him I'll ask the doctor when I see him but please hon, stay calm, it's not good for your heart to get so upset. I've never seen him like this, I didn't know what got into him. When I asked him what's wrong, he said nothing, I just want to be at home.

He asked me if I didn't want him at home. Is there something your not telling me that the doctor told you about me? No I assured him that I knew just as much as he did and that I would never hide anything from him and I was insulted that he would think I did. I tried to explain to him how I missed him terribly but we have to wait till the doctor says you can come home. We just have to be patient and go from there okay?

I changed the subject quickly talking about Amber having back pains and maybe she was in labor. I told him I talked to her and she was waiting for Mark to come home from work and they were going to see her gynecologist. She was due next week but they might of figured wrong. The baby will come when it's ready not when they think it will come. Bob was worried that Amber might have a rough time delivering since she put on so much weight during her pregnancy.

I went to the bathroom and stopped off at the nurses station to leave a message that I wanted to speak with our doctor that it was very important. When I returned back to Bob's room, a nurse was getting him out of bed to take a short walk. I kissed him good-by and told him I'll see him later. He said wait I'll walk you to the elevator but the nurse said no way you can't overdue it as far as you go is down this hall and back.

Bob looked at me with sad eyes and said next time sweetie, maybe we might even race down the hall. I told him it's a bet and left. I can't believe what this has done to Bob he was so full of life and this has taken everything out of him. I hope not for long. But everything will be back to normal in time. We will just have to take it one day at a time.

I made a quick stop at the grocery store for some items I needed but as usual I bought more then what I came in for. I ran into my friend Dolores Anderson who had lost her husband Robert We talked for awhile and she said she would pray for Bob and to give him her best. I let Queenie out when I got home and put all the groceries away.

I put the kettle on to have a cup of tea. I let Queenie back in and praised her for doing such a good job guarding the house. Went through the mail as I drank my tea and enjoyed a few cookies. I noticed Queenie needed a good brushing since I neglected her for awhile and got her brush. The minute she saw me with the brush, she came running. She loved to be brushed and her hair was very soft and shinny from it.

I called Bob at the hospital but there was no answer. I figured he was still walking slow with the nurse or was on the pot. I wrote out a couple of checks to pay some bills since I still have money in the checkbook. Lately it seemed that the money went out faster then it came in. I guess that's what they mean when they say easy come, easy go. I washed out the cup from tea, dried it and hung it on the cup hook in the cabinet. Did a fast dusting over everything and mopped the kitchen floor.

Looked at the time and figured I better get ready to go see my honey. Brushed my teeth, washed my face, put on fresh makeup, combed my hair and changed clothes. Dabbed some perfume behind my ears, grabbed my keys then left to see Bob at the hospital. I told Queenie I would be back after visiting with daddy. You be a good girl and watch the house. Traffic was light and I got there in no time at all. I stepped into the elavator and pushed the button to go up to the third floor.

When I arrived at Bob's hospital room, he was sitting up in a chair watching television. Hi, honey, look at you sitting there like King Tutt. You must of been very good since they promoted you from bed to chair. He said that's nothing, watch me go from the hospital to my house. I told him don't rush things, wait and see what the doctors tell you.

Bob said you don't understand, I miss being with you and Queenie. I want to sleep in my own bed with you next to me and sit in my own recliner. I miss your cooking, the food here is like rubber and very tasteless, even the jello is rubbery. If I stay here any longer, my heart won't kill me, the food will.

Bob said he had a surprise visit from Maryann with a friend named Mel. He seemed like a nice guy, very polite. They stayed for around an hour and bought me some magazines and candy. Mel works at the hospital and is studying to be a Gynecologist. His sister died giving birth to a beautiful daughter who only lived one day.

After that Mel told himself he wanted to save babies and to help women have healthy babies as well as themselves. Maryann told me not to get excited, they are only good friends. Of course love works in funny ways sometimes. They make a nice looking couple if I say so myself.

Bob asked me if I heard anything from Mark or Amber, but I told him when Mark knows something, he will call us. Maybe it was only gas attacks Amber was having. She has been in misery for the last few months and just wants this baby to hurry up and get out so she can be back to normal again. She said she hasn't seen her feet for almost six months. It isn't any fun carrying all that extra weight in this heat.

The nurse carried in Bob's dinner tray, no wonder he wants to go home. Heck Queenie eats better then this. It looked okay but the chicken was so dry and tough he couldn't even chew it, so he just ate the potatoes and carrots which had no taste either. He wouldn't eat the jello, he said he couldn't even look at it. He did eat the piece of angel food cake with the cup of tea and finished his glass of apple juice and a dish of pears. Now I know why he wants to come home.

I reminded him that even when he comes home, he won't be eating like before that the doctor has him on a special diet. So you will just have to grin and bear it until you get your heart. I want you around for a long time so you can't even bribe me to cook different for you. I'm following the doctor's orders. After all I'll be eating the same kind of food as you eat. It's not forever so just be patient. If you complain to much they won't release you to come back home where you belong.

On the way out of the hospital, I ran into our doctor. Boy you sure are hard to get ahold of, I've been trying to ask you if there is any chance Bob can come home? He is having a rough time staying in the hospital. He can't sleep or eat and is very crabby. I've never seen him this way and I'm scared he will have another attack or sneak out. I don't know what else to do. Bob is still very sick and not out of danger by no means. Don't forget he is working on just half a heart. He still has pain but won't admit it. We are so close that I can feel his pain in me also. I love him so much.

The doctor said he would check Bob and if things looked okay and Bob promised to behave himself and follow orders, he might release him to go home. I have your phone number and I'll call you to let you know what I have decided, one way or the other. Don't get your hopes up, after all I'm not God and can't perform miracles but I will try my best.

We want to keep Bob happy and don't want to upset him with anything right now. On the way home in the car, I thought to myself your dam right. I want my husband home with me where he belongs. I miss him dearly. Call me selfish but I want to spend my lifetime with my man not just a couple of hours.

I probably could take better care of him then any nurse since he would be my only patient. I took his vitals and gave him his medicines before so there is no problem there. I know he would be more comfortable at home with his pal Queenie at his side and better meals to eat. Heck if I had to I would even wear a nurse's uniform to make him feel better.

Maryann called and was worried about her dad coming home so soon but I told her what the doctor said and we just have to take it from there. We talked about her friend Mel. She met him at a dance and said he was a great dancer just like her dad. They were going to a movie tomorrow and planned on dropping over if it was okay. Were just friends and nothing more. I'll call you first before we come over in case dad wasn't up for company. We won't stay to long, I promise. I just want to welcome daddy home and give him a kiss.

I have to go back to work now, so I will talk to you later, love you mom. When you see dad give him a big kiss for me and tell him to get well soon. Bye for now. I had a few minutes to spare and decided to give Queenie a good brushing before I go see Bob at the hospital. The minute she saw the brush, Queenie came running over to me.

I wish someone would brush my hair for a change or even just massage my shoulders. Maybe I'll just soak for awhile in the tub filled with hot water and my lavender oil. After soaking for an hour boy did that perk me up. Now I'm ready for anything.

CHAPTER 3

▼

DOUBLE BLESSINGS

34   We Will Always Be Together

I just hung up the phone and it rang again. I thought it was our doctor calling about Bob but it was Mark. He said Amber was in true labor and couldn't talk long since he wanted to be with Amber when she delivered the babies. I told him I'm on my way but don't wait for me, go ahead, give her my love and don't worry everything will be fine.

When I arrived at the hospital, the nurse told me Mark was in the delivery room and Amber was delivering her babies. Dummy me! I never realized the nurse said babies, that means more then one baby. My God, was she having twins or triplets? I said a few prayers that Amber and the babies would be okay.

Mark walked out of the delivery room with a big smile on his face. Congratulations grandma, as he kissed me. You are blessed with not only a grandson but a granddaughter too. I kissed him and asked how is Amber? She is very tired but happy as a lark. I asked Mark how come you didn't tell me she was carrying twins? Amber made me promise not to say a word to anyone until the babies were here and everything was fine with all of them.

I can't wait to tell your father. I don't want to excite him but I think he would appreciate the good news. He will be so happy for you both or should I say all four of you. I can't wait to see the little darlings. I can't wait to hold them. Our little angels from heaven.

It's about time something good has happened, now maybe our luck has changed and Bob will get his new heart soon. Mark said come on grandma, lets go see your grandkids. We walked over to the nursery window and the nurse wheeled over two carts with babies in them. One was dressed in pink and the other blue.

God they were so beautiful and tiny. There go the tears of happiness rolling down my cheeks. I kissed Mark and told him double congratulations daddy! The babies were both sleeping like little angels. They had chubby cheeks and a lot of black hair and a beautiful smile. They were so tiny but healthy.

We both went back to see Amber. I told Mark you go ahead in I have to visit the ladies room. As he walked into her room I turned around and went downstairs to the gift shop instead of the ladies room. I found two cute outfits, one in pink and the other in blue that they could bring the babies home in. I got two rattles and a hugh balloon in the shape of a puppy.

I spotted a vase of flowers for Amber too. While I filled out the gift cards, they wrapped up the gifts. As I walked into Amber's room Mark was holding Amber's hand and they both looked like newlyweds in love. I shouted out congratulations to the new mommy and daddy and as they looked over my way they both started to laugh and asked if I bought out the gift store?

The big balloon read <u>GOD BLESS YOU TWICE, WITH TWINS HOW NICE.</u> I handed Amber the flowers and gifts and kissed her saying, good job mommy. She loved the flowers but made a fuss over the darling outfits. Oh mom, they are adorable and we can bring them home in them. Thanks mom but you didn't have to buy us anything, just being here is all we ask to help us celebrate the birth of your grandchildren.

It was the least I could do to thank you both for blessing us with our first grandson and granddaughter. I can't wait to tell your dad. I still can't believe it myself, twins! I asked Amber if she had names picked out for the babies. She said Dion Lynn for their daughter and Robert Joseph for their son. Robert was Mark's dad's name and Joseph was Amber's dad's name.

Amber's mother gave her up right after she was born, so her dad raised her with the help of her grandparents. Amber never saw her mother only pictures of her. Her dad since has remarried to a wonderful woman, Maggie. Amber's dad was in a bad car accident which left him paralyzed in a wheelchair. Maggie has her hands full waiting on him hand and foot but she loves him.

And you know when you love a person there is nothing you wouldn't do for them. Maryann had just walked in and was estatic over seeing the twins. Mark and Amber asked Maryann if she would like to be Dion's Godmother at her christening. Maryann was so thrilled and said yes, oh yes, I'd love to.

The nurse walked in and asked us to leave since they were about to bring in the babies for feeding. We both kissed Mark and Amber as we congratulated them again and left. As we passed the nursery, we glanced to see if we could see the twins but the viewing window was closed.

Maryann decided to go with me to the hospital to see her dad and give him the good news. As we entered his room, he was sitting up in a chair and I said hi, grandpa. He looked at me with a big smile and asked, you mean Amber had the baby? No, I answered, she had twins. A beautiful girl and adorable boy and all are doing fine.

Wait till you see them. They are so tiny. They named the girl Dion Lynn and the boy after you and Amber's dad, Robert, Joseph. Bob's eyes got teary as he laughed and said boy, Amber goes in the hospital and comes out with twins, I come home just with bills. Maybe I'm in the wrong hospital.

Bob said just think if I had a baby we would be rich and famous, and make all the newspaper headlines. He was worried and asked how I was holding up and was everything okay at home? I told him everything was okay except that Queenie and I missed him terribly. He said he had some good news that the doctor was in to check him out and said if I promised to behave myself and follow his orders, take my medicines and don't overdue it I could come home tomorrow.

I was so thrilled I threw my arms around him and kissed him. If the doctor was there I would probably kiss him too. Bob would have to wear a halter monitor at all times and follow a special diet. But he promised he would do everything just so he could leave the hospital and come home where he belongs. He even washed and shaved by himself and was very proud that he did it without anyones help.

A nurse walked in with some medication for him and took his vitals. I was kidding him that with such a cute nurse taking care of you, are you sure you want to leave this to come home? But he answered the only one I need to nurse me is you. Maryann said if you guys want to be alone just let me know, and we all laughed. She was so quiet that we almost forgot she was here with us.

They announced visiting hours were over so we both kissed Bob good night and told him to behave so they won't change their mind and keep him in the hospital. He said he was coming home if he even had to crawl home.

Queenie heard me pull up in the driveway and I could hear her whinning. When I opened the door she started jumping with joy to see me. I patted her head and told her good girl, then let her out in the back yard, I picked up the mail and newspaper and filled both of her bowls with fresh water and dog food. I let her back in and told her daddy was coming home tomorrow.

I swear she understood me because her tail started wagging and she looked so happy. I made myself a grilled cheese sandwich with some potatoe chips and poured a cup of coffee and took it all into the living room. I turned on the television and began to eat while going through the mail. Queenie jumped up on the couch next to me and made herself at home.

I started to pet her and realized how old she was getting like the rest of us. She still was in pretty good shape except for a little arthritis in her legs. I gave her a aspirin a day which seemed to help. She still has all her teeth which is more then I can say about myself. I wrote out a couple of bills and made a few phone calls letting our friends know Bob was coming home. I also told them the news about us becoming grandparents of twins. With all the excitement I even forgot to get the babies weight and height.

I called Amber but her line was busy so instead I called Bob. His phone rang and rang. I was just ready to hang up when I heard him say hello. He said he dozed off and didn't hear the phone. I told him I won't keep you long, I just wanted to say I love you and have a good nights sleep, grand pappy. I'll see you early tomorrow morning to bring you home. Queenie and I can't wait to have you home. You better get all the rest you can because we won't leave you alone when your home. Bye for now grandpa!

I soaked my worn out body in a tub filled with hot water and lavender oil. After feeling like a dried up prune I got out and then slipped into my lounging gown and decided to bake an angel food cake for Bob's home coming and some chocolate chip cookies for me. I baked some skinless, boneless chicken breasts with carrots for our lunch for tomorrow.

This way I will have more time to spend with Bob since all I will have to do is heat it up in the microwave. I washed out all the utensils and cleaned up the kitchen. Let Queenie out for the night and placed the cake in the cake holder to keep it fresh and the cookies in our cookie jar. Let Queenie back in and locked the door and turned off the lights.

When I crawled into bed, Queenie jumped up and laid right next to me. After a goodnights sleep I woke up to a beautiful morning and decided to pick some flowers from the garden to brighten up the house. I chose a nice assortment that smelled great and looked pretty for Bob's homecoming. I filled the vase with cold water and set the flowers in it.

There were enough flowers to put in the kitchen and living room too. I hung welcome home signs all over the house and went into our bedroom and put fresh sheets and pillow cases on our bed. The house was all set for him but now I had to get ready to pick Bob up from the hospital. I took a fast shower and got dressed. Put on some make-up and combed my hair. A dab of perfume and a quick cup of heated coffee and I was ready to go.

I let Queenie out for a potty call and grabbed a couple of cookies to nibble on while driving. Grabbed my keys and purse and let Queenie back in as I told her I'm going to get daddy to bring him home so you watch the house and be a good girl, I'll be right back and left.

Don't forget, you can't jump on daddy now no matter how happy you are to see him. You can sit by him and lick him but no jumping on him. She looked almost as happy as me to find out daddy is coming home where he belongs with the people that love him.

CHAPTER 4

WELCOME HOME

When I arrived at the hospital Bob was all dressed and packed talking to Amber on the phone. She told Bob she was bringing the babies home tonight. Mark was picking them up right after work. She told Bob to hurry and get well so you can babysit. I told Bob to ask her how much the babies weighed and their height.

Amber said Dion Lynn was 19" long and weighed 5 lbs 2 ozs. As for Robert Joseph, he was 21" long and weighed 5 lbs 7 ozs. Amber said she had to go that they were bringing the babies in for their feeding and said she would call again when she got home. I told Bob I felt bad that I thought Amber was just getting fat never realizing she was hugh because she was carrying twins.

We got Amber in good condition now we just have to work on you. God has been very good to us. Blessing us with each other, our two healthy children, a wonderful daughter-in-law and two precious, loving grandchildren to spoil. Bob was ready to go as soon as the nurse would come with the wheelchair. He said the doctor already was in to see him this morning and checked him out.

I gave the nurses a box of candy and a tray of homemade cookies to say thanks for taking such good care of my honey but that I will take over now. Bob wanted to hurry and get out of there fast before they changed their minds. The nurse finally came in with papers to sign and the wheelchair. She handed Bob papers with his diet and exercises to do, his medications and to remind him to see his doctor.

The nurse put a halter monitor on Bob that he had to wear at all times. No baths, sex, heavy lifting, running and no excitement or worry. He asked her what was left for him to do? She said he can have visitors but not for long stays, he was not to get over tired. Get plenty of rest and eat good foods.

The nurse had Bob sit in the wheelchair with one of the plants on his lap while I carried his clothes and belongings and a vase of flowers. I followed them out of the room, down the hall, down in the elevator, out the door and into the car and homeward bound. When we arrived at the house I helped him out of the car and into the house.

I sat him down in his recliner and told him not to move til I got back after unloading the car with his belongings. Queenie was so happy to see him and kept licking him as her tail was wagging so fast it looked like an airplane propeller. Bob smiled at all the welcome home signs posted all over the house. I finally got everything out of the car and into place in the house. Queenie didn't leave Bob's side for a minute.

I turned on the television and handed him all the mail and the newspapers. I asked if he was hungry but all he wanted right now was a little juice with his pills. After I got him taken care of I slipped downstairs to wash a load of his clothes.

When I came back into the living room the television was playing but both Queenie and Bob were taking a siesta.

I sat on the couch next to Bob and just stared at him. It felt good to have him home where he belongs. He looked pale and very thin. But some of my meals can put some of that weight back on. We don't want to get him to fat.

Bob wasn't interested in watching television, all he wanted to do was pet Queenie who he dearly missed. I don't know which one of us Queenie or me was the happiest to have Bob back home. It felt so good just sitting next to him and being in the same room with him. You never really miss someone until they are not around. But Bob is home now where he belongs and I'm grateful for that.

We talked about Maryann's boyfriend, Mel. The only thing we knew about him was that he reminded Maryann that he had features like her dad. Maybe that's why she liked him so much because she loved her dad. We knew nothing about him, his age, nationality, was he ever married, his religion, was this a serious relationship? Heck, we didn't even know his last name or were he lived.

Maryann did mention that he was studying to be a Gynecologist and she met him at the hospital were she worked. We will just have to wait and when Maryann is ready to tell us more, she will. I'm so happy she finally found someone nice to hang out with. I told Bob enough about Mel, how about those ever loving twin grandchildren of ours.

Mark took his vacation now so he can help Amber with the babies. Lord knows, she can use the help with everything except breast feeding. We all were walking on cloud nine. Just wait till you see those little precious babies. We were blessed twice not once. God must really love us to be so good to us.

Bob asked me if I felt old now that were grandparents? Heck no! it makes me feel lucky especially to have you because if I didn't we wouldn't of had Mark and without Mark we wouldn't have the twins. So I thank God for giving me you.

You know how Mark loves Queenie and always plays with her, well now he wants to get a puppy for the twins but Amber said to wait for awhile since her hands are full taking care of the babies. That having a puppy would be like having another baby. She's right you know, so they will get a puppy but intend to wait till the babies are at least potty trained.

Bob didn't answer me and I turned to look at him and saw he was sound asleep. I guess my talking or all the excitement of coming home wore him out. As I looked at him I could see how much he aged and even Queenie had gray hair where the black hairs use to be. I quietly went downstairs to throw the clothes in the dryer.

When I returned I covered Bob with a blanket and woke him up to take his medicine. I started dinner and put on the kettle of water for some tea. Bob went to the bathroom to wash his face and brush his teeth. While he was in there I rubbed some moisturizing cream on his back and arms. He did a few of his exercises and sat back down in the recliner. He tires so easily now.

The doorbell rang and as I went to answer it, I was surprised to see Amber and Mark with the twins. She said they were on their way home from the hospital and decided to stop off and show grandpa his grandchildren. Bob was in his glory now. He commented on how skinny Amber looked and she said here is the weight I lost although I'm still carrying it but in my arms not my stomach. Bob was amazed how tiny the twins were but how beautiful they looked. He still couldn't believe it.

Bob was afraid to hold them since he felt so weak and didn't want to drop them. He said if I know your grandma they both will be spoiled rotten. Bob held the babies little hands and asked Amber how she felt. She told him great now that it's all over. It was no fun carrying all that extra weight around and not being able to sit or stand or get a good nights sleep.

But it was all worth it and I would do it again. Mark jumped in and said oh no you won't at least not for awhile. They didn't want to tire Bob out on his first day home and they had to get the babies settled in their home too. So we all kissed everyone and thanked them for dropping over so Bob could see the babies and they left.

I asked Bob if he was ready to eat and he said he was starved. I bought in a plate with chicken and carrots and a baked potatoe. For dessert I made you your favorite angel food cake topped with fresh strawberries. I gave him a glass of cranberry juice and a cup of tea. He joked that there was enough to feed an army. But he ate everything and that made me feel good.

After he finished his meal I gave him some of his medication and he seemed to doze off. While he slept I cleaned up the dishes, fed Queenie and gave her fresh cold water and let her out. Checked on Bob who was still sleeping so I went downstairs to bring up the clothes from the dryer to fold. I let Queenie back in as she made a mad dash for the living room and sat right next to Bob. I noticed that whenever Mark came over Queenie would always play with him but not today she wouldn't leave Bob's side. Bob got up and started to read the newspaper and catch up on his mail.

Queenie barked at the back door and who walked in but Maryann with her friend Mel. She asked if her dad was still up? Sure come on in, he's in the living room on his recliner. Go sit down. I'll get us some refreshments. Mom, this is

Mel and Mel this is my mom. We shook hands and I told him it was nice to finally meet him.

Maryann walked over to her dad and planted a big kiss on him. Everyone was talking as I brought in a tray with refreshments and told them to help themselves to the cookies while I poured the coffee. Bob had a glass of cranberry juice and more of his medicine. He took one cookie to get rid of the bitter taste from the pills.

We were talking and joking around when Maryann suggested they better be going, since they didn't want to tire Bob out on his first day home. She kissed her dad and said you better listen to mom or back to the hospital you go. Bob told her the only time I will go back to the hospital is for the transplant, which would make him good for another hundred years.

I walked to the door with Maryann and Mel and kissed them good-bye. I stood and waved as they pulled out of the driveway. Bob was in the bathroom brushing his teeth. I helped him into a clean pair of pajamas, gave him more medicine and checked his halter monitor. Once he got in bed I covered him up and told him I would be right back after I let Queenie out for the night.

When I let Queenie back in, she headed right for Bob and laid on the floor by his side. Bob was already sleeping. I guess the company knocked him out. It sure felt good to have him in bed with me again. I sure missed that body next to mine every night. But now Bob is here to stay like he promised, we will always be together.

Queenie must of sensed that Bob was hurting because she didn't jump up on the bed next to him but laid on the floor by him. I could feel the warmth of his body next to mine and enjoyed the smell of his after shave lotion which I missed. I wanted to put my arm around him like we use to sleep but I was afraid it might be to uncomfortable for him so I just laid real close to him.

I turned and kissed him good night and told him I love you. I prayed to God that they would find a donor with a heart real soon. I asked the angels to watch over my darling and protect him. I seemed to fall fast asleep. We both woke up at the same time and I asked him how he slept? He said like a baby. There is nothing better then sleeping in your own bed with the woman you love.

Bob just wanted coffee for breakfast, he said he wasn't hungry. But I told him he has to have a good breakfast to keep up his strength for the transplant. I think he was afraid to eat because it hurt his chest when he would swallow. I made him some hot cream of wheat with soft toast and a glass of cranberry juice to take with his pills. He could have a cup of tea if he was still thirsty.

I told Bob that if he didn't finish everything I would take him back to the hospital personally. He grumbled something but ate everything up. See that wasn't so bad was it? More grumbling. What I didn't hear you? Nothing, he said. He wanted to bathe and shave on his own, so I let him. Yell if you need me! I left him in the bathroom and went across the hall to our bedroom to make the bed and still keep an eye on him in case he falls. I don't want to baby him but I don't want him to hurt himself either.

After getting Bob cleaned up, I helped him to sit in the recliner and turned on the television set. I covered him with a blanket and gave him a cup of green tea and the newspaper. He kept dozing off and I wasn't sure if that was normal. At lunch time he didn't want anything to eat and refused to take his medication. I didn't want to upset him by forcing him to take it, so I just called the doctor and explained the situation.

I was told to bring Bob in so the doctor could check him over. I returned back to the living room and told Bob that we had to go see the doctor to have the halter monitor checked. Our doctor was only twenty minutes from our house. I parked right in front of the entrance to the doctors office and helped Bob out of the car.

When we walked in the nurse took us right away into one of the examining rooms. Dr. Madhav came in and shook Bob's hand and asked how he felt. He checked the halter monitor and listened to Bob's heart. The nurse took Bob's blood pressure and another blood test. Dr. Madhav told Bob he has to eat or he would have to be fed through an IV in the hospital. Your medicines have to be taken at certain times and not on an empty stomach or you will really feel sick.

If you refuse to take your medicines by mouth, we will give them to you in an IV or shots. Doctor Madhav knew Bob hated needles and hoped this would scare him enough that he would take all his medicines and start eating or else he would have to face the consequences. He told me he might have to change the dosage on Bob's medicines and would let me know. Everything looks okay otherwise. Just keep on doing what your doing.

The doctor said he would call me after he got the results back from Bob's blood test. I got Bob back into the car and told him I had to go back into the office that I left my scarf in there. The nurse was nice enough to go and get the doctor. He came out and I asked him to please be truthful with me. Really how is Bob? He said he didn't want to scare him but he is getting weaker and needs that heart soon. In the meantime all we can do is pray, get him to eat, take his medicines and try not to worry.

WELCOME HOME   45

When we got home I helped him in the bedroom to get into his pajamas and back to the recliner. I made some lunch for him without even asking him if he was hungry, he would of just said no. He liked omelets with green peppers so I made that and jelly on toast, a glass of pineapple juice, a dish of sliced pears and coffee with a slice of angel food cake. This way with a choice of things he may at least eat some of it.

I couldn't believe my eyes when I came to take the tray away, he finished everything. He couldn't of given it to Queenie because she was outside. Maybe the doctor put a good scare into him about getting the IV's. He even took his medicine without any hassel. I let Queenie in and she ran towards Bob. They both fell asleep. I cleaned up the dishes and got the mail. I set it by Bob to read when he would get up. He had more get well cards from relatives. I hung all his cards up so he could see how many people cared about him besides me.

When Bob got up we watched television and talked while he continued to pet Queenie. The phone rang and it was Dave one of Bob's friends from work so I just handed the phone over to him. I went through the mail and there was a letter from Amber. I opened it and there were pictures of the twins. With a little note saying they couldn't be here with us but the pictures could take their place.

After Bob got off the phone I showed him the pictures. He was just flabbergasted at how beautiful those babies were. He couldn't wait till he was strong enough to hold them. He had plans of taking them everywhere with us. Sometimes Bob would be talking to me and fall asleep in the middle of a sentence. When he slept he looked so thin and fragile. Even his face was so pale. But with God's help and mine he would be in the best shape ever. We just have to be patient after all Rome wasn't built in a day.

Bob had so much to live for, a wife who adored him. Children who admired and loved him and grandchildren who are waiting to be spoiled by him. So many friends and relatives that like him and of course we can't forget Queenie who lives for him. The doctor called and said he was changing the dosage on Bob's medicine and explained which ones and how much starting with this evenings dosage. And to get Bob to move around more so he wouldn't end up with a blood clot. We could even take short walks.

He had to take an aspirin everyday too. I got him an electric razor so he wouldn't cut himself and bleed a lot from being on the aspirin since it works like a blood thinner. When he shaved I would kid him that it was as soft and smooth as a baby's butt. He would laugh and say that's okay just so it doesn't smell like one.

We would play cards and work on puzzles to help pass the time. I took him for short walks but it really tired him out so much. Sometimes he fell asleep with a piece of the puzzle still in his hand. I had no more problems with him taking his medicines or eating. In fact he even started to look a little better and was getting color back in his face. He would shave by himself and even bathe on his own. It made him feel good that he could do it without help from me, although I was always close by just in case he did need my help.

When bedtime came we snuggled close and always kissed good night. He smelled so tempting, he would turn me on but that's as far as it went. I had to be satisfied with just having his body next to mine for now. We fell asleep holding hands since we both were still afraid about my arm on his chest. I don't know how long we were sleeping but I had a funny feeling and opened my eyes to see Bob sitting up in the bed. I asked him what was wrong? And he said he didn't know. It was hard to explain, he just didn't feel right.

I asked him if he had any pain in his chest or anywhere else, but he just said no I just don't feel right. Instant panic grew inside me as I dialed 911. Our phone was right at my bedside so I didn't have to leave Bob to make the call. I could tell he was just as frightened as me. Bob called out my name as he held out his arms I went into his arms trying to comfort him until the ambulance would get here. He hugged me, suddenly his whole body went limp.

I couldn't feel a pulse and leaned to listen to his heart but heard nothing. The ambulance arrived and I ran to open the door to let them in and showed them where Bob was in our bedroom. They asked me to talk to the officer while they closed the bedroom door and worked on Bob. I answered the questions about Bob's health, his medications, and exactly what had happened and the time it happened. His doctor's name, his full name and age, birthday and other questions that I was asked.

I don't know why but I felt that the familar beat of Bob's heart had beat it's final beat. No matter how hard I would shake him, or how loud I would yell or cry, he would never wake up and be with me again. I stood there and prayed like I never prayed before for Bob to be okay. The medics opened the bedroom door and brought Bob out on a stretcher and carried him out to the ambulance. They didn't tell me anything except to follow them to the hospital. When we got at the hospital they hurried him into emergency.

After filling out forms again they had me sit in a small waiting room. I called Maryann and then Mark to tell them I had to rush their dad to the hospital. I told them I didn't know anything more but when I did I would call them to let them know. I knew he had died in our house. I prayed that I was wrong and he

WELCOME HOME 47

was okay. I went into the ladies room and splashed some cold water on my face and took an aspirin.

As I glanced in the mirror I saw a very old lady with tears rolling down both cheeks. I tried to pull my self together and went back into the waiting room. The hospital chaplain came in to console me and we prayed together for Bob to be okay. The doctor walked in and I could tell by the look on his face that it wasn't good news. He held my hand and said I'm sorry, we tried to bring him back but couldn't. He is in God's hands now. I started to cry real hard. This couldn't be happening to me. It must be a bad dream and I have to wake up. I felt paralyzed.

I couldn't believe that my Bob was gone, he promised we would always be together. Why did he have to die? He had so much to live for. He won't be around to enjoy his new grandchildren. What about all the plans we had of enjoying the rest of our lives together? Why Lord, did you take him from me? What will I do without him? How can I go on? I don't want to live without him, take me too.

I know Bob didn't have a choice of living or dying. Only the good ones are taken by God and Bob sure was good. I felt like someone tore my heart out of my body. Why wasn't it me instead of him? The chaplain was saying something to me, I could see his lips moving but could not hear a word he was saying. My knees started to buckle and I must of passed out, because when I woke up Mark and Maryann and a nurse were standing over me with a wet cloth on my forehead.

Maryann gave me a glass of water to drink. The chaplain had explained to Mark and Maryann that their dad didn't make it. The doctor asked if I was okay and wanted to say my last good-by to my husband? The chaplain and doctor both offered their condolences to us and showed us to where Bob's body was lying.

Mark and Maryann with tears rolling down their cheeks went in first and kissed their dad good-by. Then I kissed his lips which were lifeless and held his hands which felt cold. I told Bob not to worry sweetheart, your heart is alive and beating strong within us and your spirit is with us always. We will never stop loving you. I won't say good-by, just so long until we meet again. I love you, my darling and kissed his cold lips.

Mark and Maryann came back to my house which felt so empty right now. I realize that there is no guarantee in the hospital and that the medical profession was not always fulfilling. I know the doctors did their best but it just wasn't good enough. Only the good Lord could of saved Bob but I guess He wanted Bob as much as we did. There is no way I could make a bargain or bribe God into letting me keep my beloved here with me, Bob's time has just run out, leaving me half a person without him.

It is very fustrating and painful to experience the feeling of helplessness that occurs when everything at all possible is tried to help the patient and he still dies. It is always in God's hands and we must accept His decision no matter how much it hurts. Queenie knew something was wrong the minute I entered the house. I knelt down by her and told her daddy isn't coming home anymore.

My tears started to roll down on her hair as I hugged her and said it's just you and me now, daddy is in heaven. This felt like I was living a nightmare and just couldn't wake up from it. It just couldn't be happening to me. It was a big mistake. Maryann went in the kitchen and started to make a pot of coffee as I went in the bathroom to try and get control of my tears for the sake of my son and daughter. Mark went to the phone to call Amber and explain that his dad didn't make it.

I got out a pen and tablet and started to write down everything I had to do tomorrow. The children begged me to go and rest but I insisted I rather keep myself busy. I had to call relatives and friends and Bob's boss. Make arrangements at the funeral home, order flowers. mass at the church, the obituary column, pick a restaurant for the luncheon afterwards, pick out songs to be sung at the mass and find my papers for out cemetery plot.

I told Mark he should be home with Amber and Maryann should go home that I would see them both tomorrow. I really wanted to be alone right now. They didn't want to leave me alone but I insisted and kissed them both good-bye as they left. I went to our bedroom closet and picked out Bob's suit that he was to be buried in as the tears kept flowing from my burning eyes. How I missed my beloved partner.

I let Queenie out for the night and stayed up since I just didn't want to go to sleep in that empty bed without Bob in it. I sat there thinking, how will I survive without my better half? Death is a part of life that hurts the living and there is no way we can change that. Queenie won't leave my side, she is following me everywhere I go, even when I go in the bathroom.

Poor Queenie, I know she misses him terribly, we all do. I keep telling myself that I should be grateful that he won't suffer and is now free of pain. I know God wanted him but I wanted him too. I remember when Bob's parents and my parents died, how hard it was to go on without them in our lives, but we did. But when you lose your husband it's like losing a part of you.

Words just can't describe the feeling of emptiness. The pain in my heart feels like someone not only stabbed me in my hcart but also poured salt into the wound. There is no medicine to take away the pain. All I can do now is depend on God to help me get through my life with out my true love.

I filled the tub with hot water and lavender oil and tried to soak away the pain but it wasn't working. When I got out of the tub I looked like a dried up prune. With Bob alive I had the spirit and joy of living but now with Bob dead why should I continue to live? I sat on the couch and went through some picture albums. It brought back a lot of memories, some sweet that made me smile. Others made me laugh.

Gosh! we sure were a nice looking couple and so very happy. I fell asleep on the couch with the album still on my lap. I must of tossed all night because most of the pictures were scattered on the floor and Queenie was even laying on a couple of them, when I woke up.

Bob's death wasn't a bad dream because here I am awake but my sweetheart isn't here with me. I'm all alone with just Queenie for the rest of my life. Why do I hurt so much in my heart? Oh! Robert, why didn't you fight to live? I don't want to live anymore without you. I want to spend the rest of my life with only you my darling, even if it means my death also. Please God help me to do the right thing. Continue my lonely life or end it?

CHAPTER 5

UNEXPECTED FUNERAL

This felt like a bad dream but I knew it was real and from now on Bob would be with me only in spirit. I took a shower, got dressed and put make up on trying to cover the bags under my eyes, from crying. I let Queenie out who was waiting patiently by the back door. Filled her bowls with dog food and water. Made a pot of coffee and put the cake on the table for the family to help themselves when they arrived.

In a bag I put Bob's underwear, socks and his black shoes next to his grey suit, white shirt, striped tie that hung on a hanger on the door. In a small plastic bag I put his watch, wedding ring and a pair of cuff links, and put the bag in his suit pocket.

Mark and Maryann were just walking in with Queenie right behind them. We all kissed and sat down to have some coffee and cake and a little conversation. Mark put Bob's clothes in the car that we needed for his funeral. I put the dishes in the sink and put the cake away. Told Queenie to guard the house I'll be back soon and we all left together.

When we arrived at Sheehy & Sons Funeral home in Burbank, the entrepreneur couldn't of made us more comfortable. Mark handed him Bob's clothes and then we picked out the bronze coffin, that had a cross on each corner and a large one in the middle on the top lid. It was lined with white satin and velvet and had a crucifix inside the top lid.

Bob will be waked one day from 9:00AM to 9:00PM. They would have coffee and rolls for the people that attended the wake. I never thought I would be burying my husband at age fifty-seven. This is a nightmare and I want to wake up from it but can't.

The children and I ordered vases of roses to be placed at each side of his coffin. I handed the furneral director a copy of how I wanted the obituary column published in the Sun-Times and Southtown newspapers. I picked out some of Bob's favorite songs for his funeral mass to be held at St. Albert The Great Church with Father Stepek the officiator. We chose the Holy cards with a prayer on back that people would take in rememberance of Bob.

The entrepreneur was very helpful to us and made things go well. Everything was set Bob would be waked from 9:00AM till 9:00Pm. Father Stepek would drop by in the evening to say the rosary with us at the chapel. The day of the funeral we were to be at the chapel 9:00AM where we would say our last good-by. I chose The Burbank Rose Restaurant for the luncheon to thank the people for attending Bob's funeral. I had eight men to serve as pallbearers. The bill would be taken care of after the funeral.

We left with the funeral director saying not to worry everything will be taken care of that Bob was in good hands. Mark and Maryann have been a big help to me and I decided to take them out for lunch to thank them for being there when I needed them. No one was real hungry so we just stopped off at Bakers Square and had a sandwich with a piece of pie and coffee. Didn't stay to long. Everyone went their seperate ways.

Mark had to get home to help Amber. Maryann had to call work to explain she wouldn't be in since her dad passed away. I on the other hand had phone calls to make to relatives and friends to let them know about the services for Bob's funeral tomorrow. So we kissed and said we would talk to one another later. I thanked them and was grateful that my children were here for me at a time like this when I really needed someone around. A shoulder to cry on.

Mark and Maryann said to call them if I need anything or just want to talk. I promised them I would but right now I really want to be alone and gather my thoughts, I hope you both understand. I want to keep myself busy so I had no time to think about what really happened, that I lost my darling. Maybe then it wouldn't hurt so much.

As I approached the driveway, I opened the garage door and parked the car inside. When I opened the back door to go in the house, Queenie wasn't there to greet me. Poor Queenie, she has been so neglected since Bob was in the hospital and now this. Her best pal was never coming home to her again. She finally came walking slowly to meet me.

Hi, sweetie, were you sleeping? I let her out and she did her job and came right back in. I knelt down and put my arms around her and told her, I know sweetie, I miss him too. I promise I will try to make it up to you when all this is over. I noticed she didn't touch her food or water but then who felt like eating at a time like this.

I went in the living room and started to make my phone calls. Everyone was sympathetic and offered to help in anyway they could. I told them thank you just pray for Bob and if they could also say a little prayer for me that God can give me the strength to go on without him. My mouth hurt and was dry from talking and my eyes burned from crying to much. But I wanted to let everyone know about Bob's funeral tomorrow.

I went to the closet and picked out a black suit with a gray blouse to wear tomorrow for the funeral. I want to look nice for my honey. I got out my black purse and shoes, stockings and undies. I stuck my rosary, checkbook, a pen, hankie, gum, aspirin, my wallet and lipstick in my purse. I laid my errings and a cross necklace and watch on the dresser and the tears started rolling down my cheeks. I found a picture of Bob with Queenie and me, one of Maryann, and one with Mark and Amber with the twins. I placed these in my purse too. I would place them under Bob's pillow in his coffin so he doesn't forget us. We will always be a family of love no matter what.

Bob's death certificate was on the dresser and I picked it up and started to read it. He died of congestive heart failure. If only they would of found a heart donor maybe he would still be alive. And then again maybe not. Maybe Bob would of suffered even more. Only God controls life and death. And when our number is up He takes us whether we are ready or not. I don't think anyone is ever prepared for death. It is always a shock when one goes.

The phone rang, and it was Amber, apologizing for not coming to help me. I told her don't be silly you have your hands full with the babies. I should apologize to you for not helping you right now. We both started to cry and I told her I would call her back later since I just couldn't stop crying. After getting control of myself I continued making my phone calls till my ears hurt and my voice was hoarse. Well I finally finished to let everyone know that Bob had passed away. I sat on the couch petting Queenie. If anyone saw me talking to my dog, they would think I was nuts but Queenie isn't only a dog, she is part of our family and my best pal right now. We need each other now since Bob has gone on to the other world with God.

I noticed that Queenie still hasn't touched her dog food so I put some of the dry food in the palm of my hand to try to get her to eat but she just turned her head away. I guess death hits the feelings of animals as well as us humans if not more. I figured I would just let her be and when she got hungry she would eat. After all I should talk when I'm not eating either just living on coffee and more coffee. No one feels like eating now, maybe after this is all over we will get our appetiates back.

Right now I would love to have a cigarette with my coffee but I would never start that bad habit again. Both Bob and I smoked heavily but it's been over twenty years since we gave it up. We both felt so much better, even the food taste better. But where did it get us? Bob's dead. Maybe if he never smoked he would still be alive now. Bob promised me that we will always be together and even though he is dead, his spirit is still around me.

Since he died in this house maybe his spirit or ghost will always be here. I know his heart was badly damaged and it lacked the strength and ability to keep the blood circulating normally throughout his body. His flow slowed down causing the blood returning to his heart, through his veins to back up some of the fluid in the blood which was forced out through thin walls of smaller blood vessels into tissues. Fluids collected in his lungs and interfered with his breathing.

It even affected the ability of his kidneys to get rid of his body sodium and water. I should be thankful that he didn't suffer with a lot of pain. It was almost like dying in his sleep that's why he felt no pain and didn't know what was happening except that he didn't feel right. I fell asleep on the couch again and had a bad night trying to sleep. I guess I had to much on my mind.

The following morning I got up at 5:30 and took a hot shower. I put on the coffee and let Queenie out. She still hasn't touched her food but I threw it out and gave her a bowl of fresh dog food and cold water. I was in the bedroom getting dressed when Maryann came in with her friend Mel. I told them to help themselves to coffee while I finished dressing. As I was walking out of the bedroom Mark and Amber with the twins just walked into the kitchen.

I wore the dress Bob liked on me, errings he gave me for my birthday and a heart necklace with both our pictures in it that he gave me on Christmas. I even dabbed some of the perfume he got me, this way I felt closer to him. I kissed everyone and put the twins on my bed to continue their sleep and joined the family in the kitchen to have some coffee. Mel brought in a box of donuts for all of us. The babies started crying and Maryann and Mel took over taking care of them so that Amber could finish her milk and a donut. It looked so nice to see Maryann and Mel holding the babies as Maryann said don't get any ideas you guys were just friends.

Mark suggested we better get going, so I just put the dishes in the sink, which I could do later. I put the donuts in the cake keeper to stay fresh. Maryann got our coats and I patted Queenie on her head and told her be good, I'll be right back. Mark suggested we all get in his van since there was plenty of room. Sheehy & Sons Funeral Home was only sixteen blocks from our house so we got there in plenty of time.

The funeral director took our coats, then led us to the chapel where Bob was being waked. There were vases and wreaths of flowers everywhere. You could hear soft music playing in the back ground. We all walked up to the casket and Maryann held my hand tightly. Tears started to roll down my cheeks as I wiped them away.

God Bob looked so handsome and peaceful, it looked like he was sleeping. If you stared at him long enough, you would swear that he moved. As I leaned over to kiss him on his lips, one of my tears dropped on his lip. I had to turn away because now it was hard to control my tears. The funeral director suggested that the family take me in the room and give me a cup of coffee or water.

Amber gave me some coffee which helped me get control. I then went back in the chapel to talk with my honey while the family finished their coffee. I told them I was okay now, not to worry. Oh how I wanted to hold him tightly in my arms. Wake up honey, it's me. Bob just laid there not moving a muscle.

I still can't believe this is real and I'm waiting to wake up from a nightmare. But it's not happening. Why, oh why did you take him from me God? Things will never be the same ever. We were so happy and had so much to live for. Honey I will always love you!

Bob's hands were so cold and stiff not warm and strong like they used to be. Bob was a prankster and I was waiting for him to wake and sit up and say April Fool! or GotchYa! But it was real, he was dead and never coming back to me except in spirit. I told him how much I missed him and would never stop loving him. I said a few prayers so that God would take special care of him.

Then I walked around to see who sent the beautiful flowers. They were from his work, close friends, neighbors and family. There was even a little pillow in the corner of his coffin of white carnations and one red rose in the middle from his grandchildren. How sad that they will never know their grandpa. But I will show them pictures of him so they won't ever forget him.

There were Mass Cards in a stand from friends and relatives. I was admiring the collage of pictures with Bob and Mark and Maryann. One with his parents, our wedding picture, a picture with his buddies on a fishing trip with their big catch. Queenie his partner and pal and one of the grandkids, one with our whole family.

He looked so alive and happy on each one. People started to come into the chapel to pay their respect to Bob. As I went up to each one, they would offer me their sympathy to console me and I would start to cry all over again. I felt like I would never run out of tears. I tried to be strong for Bob and to control my crying but it was hopeless, they just kept flowing like a river.

It felt like I lost ten pounds just in water from my tears. How much more do I have in my body? So many people that I didn't even reconize.

People kept coming in, my friend Dolores with her sister Virginia, Art and his wife Rosemary, my cousin Agnes, close relatives,even our doctor was their and the priest from our parish. Many neighbors and friends that we haven't seen for a long time. The chapel was crowded with everyone that loved him. They all had such nice comforting words to say about him. I could see why, Bob was always there to help you and was easy to get along with plus he had a good sense of humor and would always make you laugh.

There wasn't one bad thing about him, that's why God probably took him. Father Stepek from our parish asked all of us to join him in prayer, as we all did. The time flew by so fast, it was 9:00 already and most of the people were gone. I walked up to the casket and leaned over to kiss my beloved good night and told him I'll see him tomorrow and walked to the back of the chapel where Mark and Amber were waiting for me with the twins.

Mel and Maryann went to get our coats. The twins were such good babies althrough the wake. Everyone stopped to admire them. They dropped me off at the house and could see that I wanted to be alone. So we kissed good night and Mark walked me to the door to see that I got in alright. I waved good by and let Queenie out. Took my shoes off and put on my house slippers. Removed my necklace and errings and put them back in the jewelry box. Slipped out of my dress and threw on my bathrobe. The house was so quiet and felt so empty and cold.

I let Queenie back in the house and put on the kettle for some hot tea. I brought in the mail and newspaper but didn't even go through it, I just laid it on the table. I gave Queenie fresh water and her food was still there. I poured the tea and went into the living room where Queenie joined me on the couch. As I was petting her I was trying to remember who was at the wake.

I couldn't even think straight, everything was happening so fast. I sat there gazeing in mid-air. My mind was a complete blank. I hated to think about tomorrow. I still have Bob here today but tomorrow he will go in the ground. I just couldn't go to sleep in that big cold bed without Bob so I just covered myself with a blanket on the couch and we both, Queenie and I fell asleep. Another restless night tossing all through the night.

No matter how tired I am I just can't sleep without Bob's arms around me or his body near me, I miss him so. I looked like death warmed over when I got up the next morning and looked in the mirror. I even scared myself with the bags under my red eyes. I put eyedrops into each eye which made them feel a little better but I still looked like hell. I even tried a slice of cucumber on each eye but it was hopeless. The only thing left now is make up to help me look normal again. I wanted to look my best for my honey. After all this will be the last day I will ever see him. Oh, that thought kills me. He promised me, we will always be together.

I always tried to look nice but today it seemed like I aged overnight. There were more wrinkles and gray hairs and it was a bad hair day for me. Everytime I combed my bangs to go left, they decided to go right. I tried to comb it all back and it would just fall forward. So I sprayed the heck out of it with good old hair spray. Well I finally looked presentable but hoped nobody felt my hair since it was stiff as a board. How could I look nice when nothing fit right. Even my clothes just hung on me after losing weight.As the coffee was perking I threw two slices of wheat bread in the toaster. Then filled Queenie's bowls with food and fresh water. I let her outside for a potty call. After awhile she started barking and I figured she wanted to come in, so I opened the door and here were Mark and Amber without the twins.

They thought it would be best to leave them home with her aunt Rosemarie to babysit. Maryann and Mel were just getting out of their car carrying a box of bakery goodies. We all sat down at the kitchen table eating the cakes and drinking coffee while conversing with one another. Mark noticed how skinny Queenie was getting. I told him she wasn't eating since Bob was in the hospital.

I said I had an appointment with our veterinarian to have her checked out. Mark said you know mom she is sixteen years old. I know but she still has good years left in her. She will be back to normal once things get back to normal and I'll have more time to spoil her. I need her as much as she needs me right now. It's just the two of us. She is lonely being home by herself with no attention given from me since I've been so busy but I will make all that up to her.

Maryann suggested we better be leaving or we will be late for Bob's funeral. I put the dishes in the sink and the cake in the cake holder. Grabbed my purse and told Queenie I'll be back just watch the house, and left. When we arrived at the chapel I asked the director if the pallbearers could wear a rose in their lapels that they would lay with their white gloves on top of the casket at the burial site. And that each person present at the cemetery would be handed a flower that they too would place on the coffin.

And to please distribute the lovely bouquets of flowers to the church and nursing homes except for the roses. I would like those to have rosaries made from them for my children and myself to remember Bob. I walked into the chapel where Bob was waked and started talking to some of the people that were there, then I walked over to the casket to say hi to my beloved and gave him a kiss. I whispered to myself that today they may take away your body but your spirit will be with me always sweetheart. I slipped all the pictures of us under the pillow that his head was resting on.

I stuck a rose in his hands that were holding a rosary. I could swear that he smiled at me. Father Stepek arrived and we all said a few prayers with him then one by one the people passed his casket to say their last good-bys. The immediate family were the last to view him. I felt my knees begin to shake and promised myself I can do it so Bob would be proud of me.

I kissed his cold lips as the tears ran down and told him so long til we meet again honey. The director took off Bob's wedding ring and handed it to me, and they proceeded to close the coffin. The tears rolled down faster and I got a big lump in my throat as I prayed to God to give me the strength to go on. From the chapel everyone met at St. Albert the Great Church were the Mass would be said in Bob's honor.

I couldn't see good because my eyes were so teary. The mass was starting and the singing sounded like a choir of angels singing. The Eulogy made me cry as it was all about Bob's life on earth and now with God up in heaven. The family he was leaving behind would some day join him when we are called by God. Now Bob was in good hands of the Lord, free of pain and is with us in spirit.

Many people received Holy Communion and when the organist played and sang the Ave Maria I couldn't control my crying as I looked up at Jesus hanging on the cross and prayed that He will help me to go on without Bob now. Father Stepek then blessed Bob's coffin and there was a procession following his coffin out of the church to our cars. We passed our house on the way to the cemetery out of respect and then went on to Resurrection Cemetery for his burial. We all gathered around his coffin at the plot where he was to be buried. It was in front of a tree since he loved trees. Mine would be to the left of his when my time would come. Bob would of been pleased to see how many people loved him and were here.

Father Stepek offered more prayers and the people joined in. I looked at the hole and it was so cold and dark that I hated to see Bob go down underground and be covered with dirt but that is Bob's wish to be buried. All the pallbearers laid their white gloves and the roses from their lapels on top of the coffin. Then the people bid their last farewell as they laid down their flowers on the coffin. The director announced that there was a luncheon being served at Burbank Rose Restaurant to please attend and handed them cards with the address of the restaurant.

The people left but the family stayed behind to watch Bob go down into the ground as I bid my last farewell. It felt like there was a big void in my life now. Your body is covered with earth and the flowers from people that love you. I'll never stop loving you and I know you will always be with me. Remember your promise to me that we will always be together, even though your body is gone I know your spirit is with me. I love you my darling forever.

My children were wonderful and never rushed me, just waited patiently until I was ready to leave. When we arrived at the restaurant many of the people were already there. The luncheon was nice and the food very good. After eating I walked around the tables to thank the people for attending Bob's funeral. Everyone was very nice and consoleing and I felt like I finally ran out of tears. After the last person left I went and paid the bill for the luncheon. There were 90 of us that attended the luncheon.

Maryann asked if I wanted her to stay with me for a couple of days till I felt better but I told her no, I will be fine and anyways you have your own life to lead especially since you met Mel. Don't worry I'll be okay. If I need you I won't hesitate to call you. I kissed them all and thanked them for being there when I needed them. I kissed Mel and told him thanks not only for the pasteries yesterday and today but for being a true friend at a time like this, thank you and God bless you.

I waved good-by as they pulled out of the driveway. As I opened the door there stood my buddie Queenie waiting to greet me. I let her outside while I went into my bedroom to change my clothes. The house was so quiet and felt so empty. I let Queenie back in and we both snuggled on the couch in the living room. I was so cold without Bob's arms around me, so I got a blanket off the shelf and covered myself up.

Queenie laid right next to me. I sat there praying to God to help me through this. I felt like I should of died with him so we could be together. Gosh! I miss him so much. Will that feeling ever go away? Queenie snuggled closer to me and shared some of my blanket. I don't know if she was cold or was trying to console me. It felt good having someone next to me even if it was my pal Queenie.

It's just you and me now pal and I promise to make up for all the neglect you had these past months. I'll be there for you and hope your there for me. It's just the two of us til death do us part.

CHAPTER 6

SURPRISING VISITS

I turned on the television not to watch it but to hear voices in the house. Even if they weren't talking to me since all I heard was the beating of my heart and the ticking of the clocks. For the past few days I was always surrounded by people but now it was just Queenie and me. I laid there thinking how people told me the pain will go away in time. Now I know what a heartache feels like. When you lose the one you love feels like someone stabbed you in your heart. The pain is unbearable and enduring. Losing my arm would of been less painful.

Everywhere I look there are memories of Bob. Even songs I hear on the radio and television were some of his favorites. Things Bob bought me, things I bought him, his clothes, his colognes, even his coffee cup which had Queenie's picture on it. I looked at our wedding picture and we were so happy. Will I ever feel like that again?? I was getting myself depressed and figured I might as well go to bed and see if I can sleep without my darling. I got under the covers and was thinking, this is where we made love, where we slept in each others arms, where we conceived our children. I can feel him near me.

I don't know if Bob is an angel, a ghost or a spirit, or if I'm imagining this because I want him so badly in my life. An angel is a supernatural messenger of God who wears a white robe, has wings and is a figure of human form. While a spirit is a kind of vapor animating the body, it's a supernatural being able to possess a person, an apparition or a specter. Whereas a ghost is a disembodied soul or spirit of a deceased person appearing to the living in bodily likeness. It's a shadowy, faint, glimmering image that floats about or haunts.

I hope Bob comes back as an angel or a spirit. A ghost might scare me. But then it really doesn't matter how he comes back, all I know is I need him in my life anyway I can get him. I finally fell asleep thinking about Bob, but had a very restless sleep missing his warm arms around me. I got up and took his robe and wrapped it around his pillow and sprinkled a little of his cologne on it. I crawled back into bed and wrapped my arms around his pillow to try and make off it was him lying next to me.

But it didn't work. It didn't have the warmth of his body. I held the pillow tightly and tried to think pleasant dreams about Bob and me. Queenie jumped up on the bed and we both fell asleep but not for long. I felt a presence in the room and it didn't feel good. I sat straight up and at the foot of my bed stood a hugh figure that was frightening.

It was dressed in a long black and deep purple robe and pointed a skeleton finger (the second finger on his-left hand) directly at me. It scared the heck out of me and I sank low under the covers and was afraid to look up again. I prayed real hard to God to protect me and asked Bob to please help me. I don't know how long I stayed under the covers but slowly I moved the covers from my head and peeked at the foot of the bed but whatever it was, it was gone now, thank God. I never saw anything so gruesome in my life not even in the movies. I hope it was just a nightmare and not real.

I know it wasn't an angel or a spirit or a ghost but whatever it was scared the witts out of me and I was still shaking. Queenie never barked or even growled at it. Maybe she never saw it or else maybe it was my own imagination. I wondered if it was evil like the devil himself or Mr. Death pointing at me to tell me I'm next to die.

I had a bottle of holy water and sprinkled the bed and the bedroom with it just in case it was something evil. I hope it never comes back again. It was odd that whatever it was disappeared when I prayed to God and asked Bob to help me. So Bob must be near and watching over me. I said a prayer of thanks and asked God to send Bob to protect me at night from strange images.

It was a pleasure to get up the next morning with Queenie licking my face. The first thing I did was check by the footboard for footprints or anything unusual like saliva stains. But there was nothing there.

It shook me up everytime I thought about what would of happened if I didn't put my head under the covers. Would I still be here or gone without a trace? I decided to forget it ever happened and went over my schedule of things I had to do today. My first stop will be to the bank and then to the funeral home to pay the bill for Bob's funeral. I plan to stop by the cemetery to put some flowers on Bob's grave and say a few prayers.

I have an appointment to see our lawyer at 1:15 and must stop off at the post office to get stamps. I still had phone calls to make. I had to notify Bob's Locals, Social Security, the Veterans, make an appointment for Queenie at the Veterinarian, and call Mark and Maryann to see how they are feeling.

If I have any time left I just might stop over to see the twins. Or maybe tomorrow might be a better day since I have so much to do today. I also have to start writing out the thank you cards to everyone. I went to put a bagel in the toaster and found two pieces of toast from the other day that I forgot to eat.

I broke it up and threw it outside in the back yard for the birds to enjoy. I poured myself a cup of coffee and smeared some cream cheese on the bagel and turned on the television to find out what kind of weather was expected for today. I gave Queenie her vitamin and took mine too. I washed the cup and saucer with the other dishes that were in the sink from yesterday. Threw a load of clothes in the washer and shook out the runners. Vacuumed the rugs, mopped the kitchen and bathroom floors, made the bed, and dusted the furniture in the living room.

I went outside to do potty patrol in the back yard. Then I turned on both sprinklers for the front and back yards. I came back inside with Queenie and watered the house plants. Filled Queenie's bowls with fresh water and dog food that she barely touched. I wrote out some bills and took Queenie for a short walk to the mail box to mail them. When I reached the corner of our block, I felt some one grab hold of my hand, but no one was around or even in sight. It was a strong grip just like Bob had when he would hold my hand. It felt so good and made me feel like I had Bob walking with us again.

Am I cracking up? Was it Bob that grabbed hold of my hand or was it wishful thinking? It didn't scare me. When we got back home I put Queenie in the house and left to do my chores. At the bank I changed the name on our accounts to my name, and drew out some cash.

From there I went to the funeral parlor. After paying the bill for Bob's funeral, the director handed me boxes of thank you cards to write out. I thanked him for the way every thing was handled for Bob's funeral. After finishing all my chores when I got back home I took off my shoes and flopped on the couch were Queenie was happy to see me and started licking my face. I let her out and checked the answering machine for messages. Mark called and Maryann called.

I got a lot done today and was proud of myself because I did it all by myself. I don't want to be a burden and be dependent on my children, they have enough to do on their own. The more I can do on my own the better. By keeping real busy it might help make the pain of missing Bob go away.

I decided to bake some cookies for the paramedics that were so nice when they came to help Bob. I baked peanut butter with nuts and double chocolate chips and placed them on a long tray and covered them with foil. I dropped them off at the firehouse while they were still warm and smelled real good. They were very grateful and said I didn't have to do that since that was their job and they were very sorry they couldn't save Bob, but they tried their best.

I told them I appreciated everything they did and this was my way to say thank you. I hope you all enjoy them and left. When I got back home I heated up a cup of coffee and enjoyed some of the cookies myself. Even Queenie enjoyed a bite or two. I wasn't very hungry and the cookies hit the spot. Queenie sure has lost the weight, you can see and feel her ribs.

I'll be glad when the veterinarian finally gives her a good check up. I hope she will be okay, I wouldn't want anything happening to her too. Poor Queenie, it's no fun getting old is it? I know she misses Bob after all he was her pal. Maybe another puppy would help perk her up and get her to start eating and putting on some weight. Or maybe now that I'm home more with her she will start eating more. I'll just have to wait and see what our veterinarian tells me after checking her out.

I gave Queenie one of her favorite treats but she just sniffed it and walked away. I tried to give her a vitamin but she refused that too. Maybe her teeth were hurting her, that would stop her from eating. I got her brush out and started brushing her. Now that she loved. If anyone heard the way I talk to her they would think I was nuts. But she does understand everything I say and has feelings just like me.

I cleaned up the mess and sat down to relax. I picked up a book "Johnny Angel" and it was so good I couldn't put it down. I got so involved in it that I never noticed how late it was until I glanced up at the clock and it was 1:45 AM, way past my bedtime. I changed into my pajamas and brushed my teeth. I put Bob's robe around his pillow and sprinkled some of his cologne on it. I slid into that cold, empty bed next to his pillow with my arms wrapped around it.

I fell fast asleep. No monster, no nightmares, just a deep dreamless sleep. When I got up the following morning for some reason I just couldn't get started and it seemed like I was doing everything in slow motion. I called Queenie to let her outside but she didn't come. So I called again but still no Queenie. I thought maybe I forgot to let her in the house last night but remembered I did, then locked up. I checked in the bedroom and she wasn't there either. I looked in the kitchen and not a sign of her.

I walked into the living room and she was there lying on the couch. Her eyes were open and she was looking right at me but she wasn't moving, even when I called to her. I touched her and she still didn't move. I placed my hand on her chest to feel her heart beating but no movement at all. I picked up her left paw and it was limp. I started crying and went to the phone and called Mark. I explained what had happened to Queenie and Mark said he would be right over and hung up.

I covered Queenie with a blanket and just waited for Mark to get here. When he got here, he lifted Queenie wrapped in the blanket and laid her gently into his van. We drove to the Crestwood Emergency Veterinarian. Queenie was laid on a steel table in the examining room. The veterinarian said Queenie must of died in her sleep from a stroke and her age was of no help. I couldn't control myself and burst out crying. Mark had his arm around me as the vet handed me a kleenex and said they would handle the cremation of her body. I hated to see her go she was such a good dog and true friend but I know she wanted to be with Bob.

I gave her a good-by kiss and thanked her for sharing sixteen of her wonderful years with me. I told her I hoped she and Bob would be very happy together and someday we will all be together again. Why is God taking away everyone I loved? First Bob and now Queenie. I have no one anymore just me. Lord do you hate me so much that you are punishing me this way? Will I ever be happy again or am I next to leave this world?

I'm begining to even hate this house. It's like all of a sudden bad things are happening to me. First Bob then Queenie, who will be next? This house use to be full of laughter but now there is just sadness. It will never be the same ever again.

CHAPTER 7

LIVING ALONE

The emergency veterinarian handed me the blanket that Queenie was wrapped in and her collar with her name tag, rabies tag, dog license tag and a medal that was suppose to protect her from harm. I guess it didn't protect her from death. He handed me another kleenex because the tears were still running down my cheeks. Mark still kept his arm around me for support and asked me if I wanted a drink of water, which I said yes please.

I drank the water with an aspirin I had in my purse. I blew my nose and took a deep breath and it did help to control my tears. I paid the bill and left with Mark and got into his van. I was surprised because instead of taking me home, Mark drove me to his house to visit with Amber and the twins.

It was nice to spend time with those little angels. They were so precious, happy and full of smiles all the time. Amber was a good mommy to them as well as a good wife to Mark. She had her hands full taking care of all of them and the house. Amber was a great cook and loved to bake just like me. The house was spotless and you could smell apple pie baking in the oven.

She cut each of us a slice of pie and added ice cream on top with a cup of coffee to wash it down. It was the best medicine I needed right now with Queenie dying. I appreciated both the food and the company too. After enjoying playing with the twins and they were to take their naps, I asked Mark to drive me home. We kissed good-by and I returned back to my empty, cold house.

Mark dropped me off and waited for me to get in the house and turn on the lights. He didn't stay because he was needed at home to help Amber with the twins. I thanked him for being there when I needed him. And also for sharing his family with me today, I sure needed that. He kissed me good-by and said that's what families are for, you taught me that.

Please mom, don't hesitate to call on us when you need anything even if you just want to talk. And don't be a stranger drop over any time you feel like, we love to see you. Got to go, love you! And I waved as he pulled out of the driveway. It felt odd to open the door and not see Queenie there waiting to greet me. Here we go again, the tears are running down my cheeks. Her bowls still were full of her dog food and water that Queenie never touched,

I emptied them, washed them and put them away with all her doggie toys and brush. I stored it all in a box and put it in the crawl up stairs. It was so quiet in the house you could hear a pin drop. I was begining to hate this house and my life. It felt like I was hexed. What's the sense of even getting up in the morning, I have nothing to live for. I don't have to cook or clean for anyone anymore, not even my dog since I don't have one anymore.

LIVING ALONE   69

How will I survive? I guess I will just have to adjust and learn to live alone. Other women did. I must admit I was mad at God for ruining my happy life but then He was the one who gave me this happy life. Things always happen for a reason, I don't know why. But maybe someday I will find out the reason. I just have to shut up and deal with whatever God has in store for me. There are many people that are worst off then me. No food or family or even a house to live in. So I count my blessings.

After all God had provided me with great grandparents the best parents, a wonderful husband, loving children and now beautiful grandchildren and a love-able daughter in law, even a caring friend, Mel. I've been blessed with many good friends and relatives, good health and did have a wonderful dog Queenie. When I count all the good things God gave me I can't really complain. There are so many people out there who are less fortunate and never got to know what love or happiness was.

I'm sorry God, I don't mean to take it out on you. I thank you from the bottom of my heart for all you have blessed me with in all these years, and please take good care of Bob and Queenie and my other loved ones up in heaven with you. Help me, oh God to cope with living a normal life once again, and to heal this ache in my heart. Make me strong so I can manage on my own and not be a burden to my children.

I wasn't any good for visiting friends or relatives yet. Until I get rid of all my tears and pain. I'm no good to anybody. I just have to keep myself busy and I can start now with writing out the thank you cards. The children asked to help me but it would be hard because I wanted to write something special on each one and they wouldn't know what I wanted to write. This is what I needed to do on my own. It should take my mind off crying. And with all the cards I had to write out I would be to busy to have time for pain or lonliness.

I kept myself so busy that I didn't even know what day it was. Months passed and I was busy doing anything and everything. I worked on crafts, took up reading books, doing puzzles, gardening and I even took a computer class although I didn't even own a computer. I visited with the families and talked without shedding tears. I played with the twins and Amber and I would take them to the park on the swings. They were getting into everything now. Bob sure would of loved playing with them.

I would go shopping and out to lunch with Maryann. I always found time to see my honey at the cemetery. I started to go on trips from our Park Districts, and enjoyed them. As I got up every morning I would exercise for one hour on the threadmill and then do my regular exercises. Every Saturday I attended mass at 5:00 and received Holy Communion at St. Albert the Great Church.

I washed windows, painted the rooms inside the house, mowed the lawns, planted a flower garden and a nice size vegetable garden. When it didn't rain I would sprinkle our lawns at 6:00 in the morning. I always got up early like 5:00 no matter what time I went to sleep which was usually after 1:00 AM.

I kept in contact with my friends and relatives through mail or by phone. Always remembered birthdays, anniversaries, and holidays with cards and gifts. Kept in close contact with my family, they are all I have left now and I love them dearly.

As I finally started to get comfortable on the couch, I felt sick to my stomach. I made it to the bathroom just in time and felt like I would never get off the potty. With all my vomiting you wouldn't think I had anything left inside of me but I sure did. I spent half the night in the bathroom. Now I know what they mean when they say a good clean out. I was squeekie clean inside and was ever so hungry.

I sure could go for a Subway Sandwich only this time a footlong instead of a six incher. Even a nice banana split would hit that empty spot. It's funny how hungry you get when you know you can't have anything to eat. I thought everything was out of me but I was wrong.

My poor butt was sore already but it finally stopped since everything was drained out of me. I felt weak and very tired and mostly very hungry. I could eat a horse not even cooked. I figured I couldn't get food off my mind so I decided to call it a day and retire early. Tomorrow will be a busy day. I covered myself with the comfortor and felt snuggly. Before I knew it I was fast asleep and never got up once until the alarm went off at 4:30 AM.

I took a nice warm shower and brushed my teeth. Got dressed and combed my hair, another bad hair day. I picked up yesterdays newspaper and the mail which I forgot to bring in when I got home last night.

I didn't cook to much since there was only me but I would fix a darn good meal when the family came over for the holidays. I baked a lot and gave it away to my kids and some of the neighbors. There were times I was so busy that I just forgot to eat. I tried hard to dream about Bob and Queenie but it would never happen. I know Bob is here with me because I can feel his presense.

I was sitting in the living room and I could swear I saw Bob sitting on the arm of his recliner, smiling at me but I blinked and he was gone. Anytime I heard a strange noise or when the lights blinked, I would ask, is that you Bob? If anyone heard me they would probably call the men in the white coats to get me.

While washing a load of clothes downstairs, I noticed I was standing in a puddle of water and you could see it pouring out from a hole in the elbow under the utility tub. You should of heard me trying to get the old elbow off so I could take it with me to get the right size.

I couldn't budge it, I twisted, banged, pulled and turned but it wouldn't budge one bit. I got angry and yelled, it's all your fault, Bob it's your job to fix things not mine. I even kicked the elbow. Then as if Bob was there helping me, the elbow turned so easy and I got it off. I went to Ace Hardware and purchased a new one. I use to watch Bob do repairs and help him so I knew a little about what to do.

When there was something that I didn't know how to fix, I would read books on how to fix things and believe it or not I got it done. If it was something big that I knew I couldn't do well then I hired a repairman who knew what to do.

I put plumbers tape around both ends of the elbow and installed it, and tightened the fastners on each end. I ran the water full force to see if it was dripping anywere but it was as good as new. I then apologized for me yelling at Bob because I knew he was here to help me fix it. I knew he wouldn't let me down.

I wish I could find a Genie in a bottle or a lamp and rub it to see my husband and Queenie anytime I wanted to. But that only happens in the movies. Only God can make anyone appear or disappear if He wanted to. I was very proud of myself that I fixed the pipe without having to bother the children. I'll bet even Bob was proud of me. It's funny but when things have to be repaired and there is no one around to do it, how fast you learn to fix it yourself.

I have learned to be a plumber, a electrician, a painter, gardener, business manager and whatever. I know Bob is here helping me to do things even though I can't see him, I can feel him. When I couldn't find things that were misplaced, it was like a little voice told me where to look in that drawer or in the closet and sure enough that's where I would find the article I was searching for.

I never expected Bob to die so young. We use to kid each other about going out when we were old in our wheelchairs, racing down the streets together with Queenie following. I guess that won't ever happen since they are no longer with me except in spirit only.

Death strikes anyone at anytime. It takes the old as well as the young, and some that weren't even born like in a miscarriage or stillborn. We are never prepared for it and just have to accept death as we do life. But it isn't easy to handle the pain and lonliness from it. I often wonder if Bob had the heart transplant would he still be alive. There are many people that had new organ transplants and died on the operating table or a few months later. When your number is up nothing can change that. There is no way one can hide from death.

I just keep telling myself that now he is in peace without pain and with God and my loved ones. I'm just grateful that we had years of happiness with each other, and were blessed with our children. It's ashame that he won't get to play with his grandchildren. I will try to make up for his absence with them. I know he is having fun with Queenie up in heaven. Maybe it isn't wise to love someone that much because then it wouldn't hurt that bad when they are gone.

The pain never goes away with time as people tell you. It's still like there is a big hole in the center of my heart that I can't seem to fill with the love that once was there. Don't get me wrong, I do love my children and grand children but it is not the same as the love I had for my beloved husband. Only one that has lost a mate knows what I am feeling. Emptiness and pain.

My relatives and friends tell me to find a good man and marry again but I can't see falling in love with someone else. I could never love anyone as I loved Bob. If God wants me to marry He will find a man for me, I put my trust in Him. I have learned to take it one day at a time. It is a very lonely life compared to what I had.

The daytime it's okay because I keep myself busy, especially with the twins but when night rolls around and you sleep by yourself you wonder if it is worth being alive. I still miss Bob something terrible, I guess I always will. He was an important part of me. I feel like a machine that has a part missing just doesn't work well or at all.

I see myself ageing right before my eyes. My face has more wrinkles each day, my red hair has turned to gray and even the texture has changed from smooth to wirey. My ears seem larger and I even have gray hair in my eyebrows. Those long sexy eyelashes I once had are now gone. My hairline is receding which I thought only happened to men. The bags under my eyes are so big even cucumber slices don't help anymore, maybe I need to use the whole cucumber.

My once slim, sexy body now looks like my mother's not mine. I lost a lot of weight and with age the elasticity is gone so the skin just hangs no matter how much exercise I do. My bosom which was something to be proud of now I can wear shopping bags instead of a bra. Maybe it's good that Bob isn't around to see me this way. He always said I was the most beautiful woman in the world and if God made any woman better then me He probably would keep her for Himself.

I'm falling apart slowly. My legs don't work right and my fingers are getting crippled from arthritis. And my eyes aren't what they use to be, the glasses keep getting thicker for me to see good and I have a cataract in my left eye.

My appetitate has really gone downhill. I've caught myself eating one meal a day and that would consist of a sandwich or a piece of cake or pie or cookies with coffee. I just don't enjoy eating by myself and I don't feel hungry. I get around five hours of sleep a day but I'm just not tired. Some people don't need much sleep and I must be one of them. The children keep yelling at me to eat and to go see our doctor for a check up. He would probably give me something to get an appetiate and eat, and something to make me sleep.

I got on the scale and from 176 lbs I've dropped down to 120 lbs. Maybe that's why I feel fatigue all the time. My kids tease me that I wear a girdle to keep my bones from rattling. To keep peace in the family I called and made an appointment with our doctor. He could see me tomorrow at 11:30. The nurse asked me what was the problem for seeing the doctor. After explaining about the weight loss and no appetiate, she told me to fast that the doctor would probably want to do a blood test.

I decided to drop over and play with the twins and give Amber a rest. They were up and playing with their toys. I sat down on the floor with them and joined in. Gosh Bob would of really had fun playing with them. They were so cute and would make me laugh. When you sat inbetween them it was like sitting with matched bookends on each side of you. They would make funny faces and sounds and loved throwing toys. I loved them so much I could eat them up, they were adorable.

They both had big brown eyes and dark brown hair and plenty of it that they could use a haircut especially Robert Joseph. He could pass for his sister Dion. They both had the cutest smile and I loved to hear them giggle. The babies were getting hungry so Amber handed me Dion to feed while she had Robert. It felt so nice to hold such a little darlings. I put her on my shoulder to burp her and she put her tiny hand around my neck and began to slobber all over my face like she was trying to eat my face.

I kept patting her back lightly until she let out a big burp that sounded like it came from her toes up. Amber and I laughed because by no means was she a lady and then she farted. Dion didn't smell to good so Amber took her to change her and handed me Robert. He was full of smiles and started to grunt, well you know what that meant. I carried him into the bedroom and Amber just got through with Dion and handed her back to me as she changed Robert.

Boy how good they smelled now with powder and a clean diaper. Dion started rubbing her eyes as I rocked her in the rocker. She fell asleep and I laid her down in her crib. Amber put Robert in his crib and suggested we go in the kitchen and have lunch. I told her I wasn't hungry but I would have a piece of the apple pie she just baked. As she cut the pie she asked me if I was alright since I looked like hell. I told her I was seeing my doctor tomorrow.

The doctor will probably just give me some pills to build up my appetiate and something to make me sleep better. She asked me to stay for dinner but I told her I couldn't but planned to make it for another time. I looked at my watch and told her I better be going and thanked her for the nice get together and kissed her good-by and left.

It was close to 6:30 and I knew Maryann would be home from work so I thought I would surprise her and drop over. I rang the bell but there was no answer, I rang again and started to turn around to leave as the door opened. Mom! what a nice surprise, come on in. Something smelled awful good and in the kitchen there was Mel, with an apron on, cooking dinner for them. Hi, he said your just in time for dinner.

Sit down and join us there's plenty. It smells lucious and looks great but I just ate at Amber's but I will have a cup of coffee if you have any. For you we would make some special. Maryann started with I suppose your wondering what Mel is doing here in a apron. Well mom, you might as well know that Mel and I are living together. My room mate left and got married and I couldn't afford to pay the payments so seeing that Mel and I got along so well and we were seeing each other everyday, Mel decided to move in and help with the payments. He is a wonderful cook as you can see and a better housekeeper then me. And so far it's working out great. And both of us are saving money and learning a lot about each other. I couldn't ask for a more trusting room mate.

CHAPTER 8

HAPPY MEMORIES

This is 2006 and a lot of grown ups are living together nowadays. In a way it's like a test to see if you both can get along with one another living under the same roof. Maybe if more people tried this there wouldn't be so many divorces. If this works out for us, who knows what it may lead to. I might as well tell you the other news as Maryann showed me her left hand that had a ring on her finger. We were engaged and were planning to tell you but couldn't find the right time since dad died.

We both didn't know how you would feel about it so we decided to wait to tell you. I just couldn't tell you such happy news when you were so sad. I ran and kissed Maryann and Mel and congratulated both of them and said that was the best news I've heard in a long time. I'm so happy for you both and I know your dad is too. I wished you would of told me sooner it would of helped me feel good.

Have you set a date to get married yet? I'm so excited for you I can't tell you how pleased I am to have you Mel in our family. I told them they didn't have to wait to get married on my account, they have my blessing to get married today if you want. Does Mark and Amber know? We didn't tell anyone yet. We wanted you to be the first to know the news.

Tears started rolling down my cheeks, but this time they were tears of joy. Mel and Maryann had an appointment at St Albert The Great rectory to speak with Father Stepek about setting the date for them to get married in church. They both wanted just the immediate family and not a big wedding. Mel's parents if they could make it, Amber and Mark, Mel and Maryann and me besides the priest who would be marrying them.

They wanted to get married on August 31st that was the day they met. But wouldn't know for sure until they talked to Father Stepek. It was getting pretty dark out and I didn't leave any lights on in the house so I told them I better get going. They both walked me to the door and I invited them over for lunch tomorrow but they had other commitments and took a raincheck for another time. I congratulated them and gave them both a kiss good by and told them how happy they made me.

When I walked into the house it was dark and cold and very quiet. I turned on some lights and the television. Then went to collect the mail and newspaper. Sat down on the couch in the living room and started thinking that now even Maryann will have someone to love her. Mel was meant for her, even Bob and Queenie liked him. You could see it in their eyes how much they loved each other. I hope they will be as happy as Bob and I were but that they can be together a lot longer then us.

You could tell Mel loved Maryann by all the things he does for her that he didn't have to. And he loved children you could tell by the way he was always playing with the twins. He even changed their diapers. How many men do you know would do that? They both love children and I hope they are blessed with many since they both would make great parents. I couldn't be any happier for them, they deserved it.

Maryann is awful pretty and Mel is very handsome, so their kids should be adorable. Listen to me I already have a family for them and their not even married yet. Bob would of been honored walking Maryann down the aisle to give her away to Mel. It's another thing he missed through no fault of his own. I fell asleep thinking good and happy things for a change.

When I woke up I was still in my clothes from yesterday and on the couch. I took a shower and got dressed. I didn't have to make the bed since I didn't sleep in it. The phone rang and it was Maryann asking me to go shopping with her to pick out a wedding outfit. She didn't want a gown and veil, just a suit or nice dress and hat to match. I told her fine but it would have to be after 1:00 since I have a doctor's appointment.

It would work out great for her too so we agreed to meet at 2:00. I went back into the bathroom and loaded moisturizer on my legs, hands, neck and face. That moisturizer just soaked in my skin like water in a sponge. I turned on the television and read the newspaper since I couldn't eat or drink anything because of the blood test the doctor would take. Why do you always feel so hungry and thirsty when you know you can't eat or drink anything? I would just have to get my mind off of food and think or do something else. It was only 9:00 so I decided to go to Kohl's to kill time.

When I went into Kohl's, there were only a few customers that were shopping. I guess people were at work or still sleeping. I found two adorable outfits for the twins. Pretty pajamas for each one and some musical wind up toys that had flashing lights and made different musical tunes. I just know they would love them and if not I could play with them when I go over there to see them. The colored lights flashing to the music that played would attract any child.

I picked out a nice card for Mel and Maryann on their engagement, signed it after I paid for everything and put a stamp on it and in the mailbox it went. I also bought a beautiful wedding card for them but that I left in the bag with my other purchases since I won't be needing it for awhile.

I glanced at my watch and figured I better get going or I'll be late for my doctor's appointment. I hurried to my car and headed for the doctor's office. As I entered into the waiting room it was pretty full. I signed my name, grabbed a magazine and found an empty seat until they would call me. There were four other doctors in this building so maybe it would go fast. I finished the magazine and took another one. Halfway through it, the nurse called my name.

I followed her into the examining room. She weighed me, 115 lbs. Took my blood pressure, 181/61, took my pulse and then asked me a lot of questions and wrote down my answers. She handed me a gown to put on after I removed my clothing, keeping my panties on. She said the doctor will be in shortly and left the room. It sure felt cold in the room and seemed like I was waiting a short time. Why do the examining rooms always feel so darn cold especially when you have your clothes off?

I waited around ten minutes and then the doctor walked in. He said I see by the chart your not feeling to good, well lets see if we can make you feel better. He checked my mouth, ears, listened to my heart and chest and back, felt my pulse, checked my ankles, pressed all over on and around my breast and under my arms. Even checked my eyes. He took two vials of blood from my arm. Told me to get dressed and he would be back to talk to me. When he returned, he handed me prescriptions to get a mammagram and chest X-Ray at the hospital and to make an appointment for a pap smear from my Gynecologist.

He gave me pills that should increase my appetite and another that would help me sleep. He told me that I was very anemic because even the white in my eyes were yellow. He wouldn't prescribe anything else until he got the results back from my bloodwork. He scolded me for not eating and said sometimes you have to force yourself to eat in order to survive. He said, are you trying to kill yourself? I promised to eat more and made another appointment for next week.

I left and went to CVS Pharmacy to get my prescriptions filled. After waiting twenty minutes they were ready, so I paid for them and returned home. I kept thinking what the doctor had said. Are you trying to kill yourself? Was I trying to kill myself and not even know it? I wanted to be with Bob because I missed him but I'm not ready to die. Not with Maryann getting married and enjoying my grandchildren that I simply adore.

I want to spend time with my children and grandchildren. I plan to be around and see my only daughter getting married and living happily ever after. And who knows, God might bless me with even more grandchildren to enjoy. I have a lot to live for now even though I do miss Bob a lot and always will.

I took a ride by Amber to drop off the twins clothes and toys but they weren't home so I just left the packages inside the enclosed porch with a note attached. When I returned back home I had just enough time to freshen up as Maryann pulled in the driveway to pick me up for our shopping spree. From the time I got into the car our mouths never stopped working.

We laughed and talked so much that my mouth hurt, but it was a good hurt. It's been awhile since I spent time alone with my daughter and we were having fun doing things together. Maryann told me they saw Father Stepek and everything was set for August 31st at 5:00. I was so happy for her that I leaned over to give her a kiss and almost caused an accident.

Mel's parents wouldn't be able to attend the ceremony since his dad isn't in the best of health and is on oxygen and a lot of medicines. So Mel and Maryann will stop over to see them in Arizona after their honeymoon. Mark and Amber will be our witnesses as well as the best man and my maid of honor. We aren't having a reception just a small luncheon with the five of us at The Flame and Father Stepek if he can make it. I reminded her that her dad would be there because he wouldn't miss his only daughter's wedding. But he will miss giving her away to Mel.

After checking out a couple of stores Maryann finally found the perfect suit to wear at her wedding. It fit her perfect and the color pastel peach was great with her complexion and hair color. It even had a cute little hat with a short veil that matched. We found a pair of shoes and a small handbag that matched perfectly.

I even found a light beige outfit for myself, since nothing fit me right after losing so much weight. I paid for everything and told Maryann it was part of her wedding gift from her dad and me. Our feet hurt and our bellies needed food so we stopped off at The Flame to have lunch. We enjoyed a bowl of cream of broccoli soup and a salad and even had a toast to her wedding with a glass of white wine.

I told her how happy I was for her and that Mel was good husband material, that I was proud to have him for my son-in-law. It was time to get on with the rest of our shopping. Maryann found some real sexy nightwear to knock Mel off his heels. Maryann dropped me off at my house and kissed me, thanking me for everything, especially for being her mom.

When I walked into the kitchen, I noticed the answering machine was flashing. There was a message from Amber saying she found the toys and clothes for the twins and loved them. The clothes are a perfect fit and the toys, well what can I say. The twins are having fun with the colored, flashing lights and the music. I like it myself.

You always seem to get things they love. You should see them trying to dance to the different sounds. I wish I had a camcorder to catch them on film. They sure are enjoying that toy. They will probably burn it out from playing it so much.

Amber said the twins couldn't take their eyes off the flashing colored lights and those different tunes it played was fascinating and caused them to dance to the musical tunes. You always seem to get them things they like. It should wear them out completely and make them sleep better. They sure are lucky to have a grandma like you. Thanks mom from all of us, love yah, bye.

Busy, busy, busy that's my middle name or should I say dizzy instead of busy. I was so tired from shopping that I just flopped my whole body in bed, clothes and all and fell fast asleep. I'd swear I heard Queenie barking to go outside and jumped up from bed to find out it was only a dream since Queenie was in doggie heaven. I looked at the clock and it was only 4:31 AM but I wasn't tired anymore so I stayed up and filled the tub with hot water and my lavender oil to help me relax.

I sunk in past my shoulders and closed my eyes and put my head back just thinking happy thoughts. I asked Bob if he wanted to come to his only daughter's wedding with me? It brought back memories of our wedding. Gosh we were so happy and young. I hope Mel and Maryann will be as happy as we were and that they will have a long life together with a lot of children.

After feeling like a prune from soaking so long I got out of the tub, dried off and rubbed my moisturizing cream all over my body. Today I had no plans of going out.

I just wore a sweat shirt and pants and put my hair in a pony tail. I decided to bake some raison bread and a coffee cake. I may not eat good food but I love to eat baked goodies. I guess I'm a pastry freak. Give me cake, candy and ice cream and you can keep the rest of the food. I know it's not good for you but then look what Bob ate, all healthy food and his vitamins and supplements with plenty of exercise. No smoking or drinking and where did it get him? In an early grave.

I'm going to enjoy life so when I go I'll have a big smile on my face. After I finished baking I went outside in the back yard to make a planter for Bob's gravesite. I put a few stones on the bottom of the planter and filled the rest with top soil. In the middle I planted a spike and put red geraniums on each side, then filled the rest of the planter with white snapdragons and violet petunias.

I printed Bob's name on the front and back with a pernament black marker and glued a reflecter on each side. It looked pretty, hope he likes it. I watered it good and set it in the sun and started to do the planters for Bob's parents and mine. When I finished all of them I did some weeding in the flower and veggie gardens. My back was hurting I guess I'm not as young as I thought I was.

I noticed it's getting harder to do a lot of things as I get older although I would never admit it to my kids. I went back inside the house, cleaned up and grabbed a book to read but I just couldn't get into reading it. I decided now was a good time to clean out Bob's closet but I still couldn't do it. As long as his clothes were here I felt he was still with me. I even wear some of his shirts to make me feel close to him. I'm just not ready yet to clean out his closet. Who knows maybe I never will.

I even tried to clean out his drawers from our dresser but I just couldn't bring myself to get rid of anything that belonged to him. I picked up his wallet with our pictures and it still had money in it. Everything is just the way he left it. His watch, wedding ring a medal of Christ on a chain, all his colognes on a silver tray. It felt good to touch his things when I dusted around them.

I put his wedding ring on a chain and put it around my neck under my sweat-shirt. I would do anything I could to make him feel close to me. After I finished my work I sat down in the living room where I pulled out the picture albums and went down memory lane again. I came to our wedding pictures and we looked so much in love with each other, we sure did make a nice looking couple.

There were pictures of our vacations, the children baptized in church, their graduations, our parents, Queenie, Mark's wedding, Bob's fishing trip with the guys, Christmas when Bob played Santa Claus, our Thanksgiving dinners with the families. Bob in his uniform when he was in the service, gosh he sure was handsome.

I was very lucky that he noticed me with all the cute girls that were around. When I came to the twins pictures, I noticed how much Robert Joseph resembled Bob when he was a baby on his pictures. There were so many pictures of the good times we shared like in our swimming pool in the back yard. Pictures at parties with our friends, even some from the amusement park in Monticello Indiana. I have all these precious photos and the memories that no one can take away from me. Plus I have the memories of Bob in my mind and in my heart that there are no photos of just a pleasant memory.

The last picture I have of Bob was when he came home from the hospital and sat in his recliner. He looked very sickly on it and I kissed the picture. I didn't want to get depressed so I laid down the album and picked up a book to read instead. I started to read but just couldn't get into the story.

I decided to take it back to the library and get a different one. I looked in my purse for my library card but it wasn't there. That's where I always kept it. I checked by the phone and the mail then on my dresser but still couldn't find it. A voice told me to check my pocket in my blue jacket. Sure enough that's where it was.

Thanks Bob, for helping me find it. While walking to the library I could feel that I wasn't alone. It felt like Bob was right beside me holding my hand like he always use to. I could feel the warmth of his hands going right through mine. What a wonderful feeling. Bob was always around when I needed him just like when he was alive.

If I was falling, he was there to catch me. We were like salt and pepper, bread and butter, bacon and eggs, coffee and cake. Some people are like water and oil, they just don't mix well but we were like soap and water and mixed together perfectly.

At the library I found two books to check out. "Life On The Otherside" by Sylvia Browne and "One Last Time" by John Edwards. They both communicate with the dead. Now maybe by reading their books I will be able to communicate with Bob and my loved ones. If I could talk with him just once I would be happy. I just want to know if he is okay and misses me like I miss him.

I fell asleep while reading and when I woke up the book was on the floor and I even lost my page where I left off. I looked at the time and hurried to get washed and dressed to keep my appointment at the hospital for my Mammagram and Chest X-Ray. There was nothing to the x-ray but there should be an easier way to get a Mammagram. After your breast is flattened upwards, downwards and sideways you really wonder how you will get your square bosoms into a rounded brassiere.

It seems to hurt more as you age, probably because my bust has gotten bigger and the elasticity is gone. After leaving the hospital I decided to stop off at the paint store to get some swatchs. I wanted to paint the kitchen a brighter color. Just as I walked in the back door, the front doorbell was ringing.

I ran so fast that I almost tripped on my own feet. I opened the front door and there stood a delivery man with flowers that had my name on the card. I accepted them and gave the man a tip as I thanked him. I took them into the kitchen and wondered who could of been sending me flowers? It couldn't be from Bob, I found a card inside the beautiful bouquet. It read Thanks Mom for everything, especially for being my mom, Love Maryann.

They were not only pretty but smelled great. It was just what the kitchen needed to brighten up the place. It felt nice to receive flowers again. It's been a long time since I got flowers or candy or perfume from Bob. He would get me things for no occasion at all. He would say I got you this because I love you. I

HAPPY MEMORIES 83

miss those little gifts from him, I guess I got spoiled from him. And he sure believed in spoiling me. God I wish he was here with me, I miss him so much.

I dialed Maryann's number and she answered on the second ring. Thank you so much for the beautiful flowers but you didn't have to do that. I enjoyed buying you your trousseau and spoiling my only daughter. Maryann said she just wanted to show me how grateful she was. Here I go again, teardrops from heaven. I wish I could control my crying but I've tried and it's impossible.

I cry when I'm happy like now and when I'm sad, I guess I'm just a sentimental and emotional mom. Thanks again I love you, and then I hung up. I went downstairs to wash a load of clothes and bed sheets and cases. Threw them in the dryer and went back upstairs and made a tuna sandwich on rye and some cottage cheese with peaches. I finished it off with a cup of coffee and a piece of coffee cake. Took my pills and went into the living room and turned on the television.

I watched "Ghost" again. I love that picture and never get tired of watching it over and over. I gave Mark a call to see how everyone was doing. He said the twins were into everything and Amber really has her hands full chasing them all over the house. I asked him if she needed help but he said no she wants to do everything herself this way she stays thin. We didn't talk to long because Amber was getting the twins ready for a bath and Mark helped her out. So I cut it short and gave them my love and said to give the twins a kiss from me. I folded the clothes from the dryer and called it a day.

The phone rang early in the morning and I was still in bed. It was the nurse from the doctor's office asking me if I could come in today to see the doctor, that he received my results from my tests. I told her no problem, that I could get there in around an hour. I showered fast, got dressed, combed my hair, brushed my teeth put on some make up to help me look alive and a dash of perfume so I would smell pleasant.

It was ten oclock when I got to his office. There were three patients before me. I felt sick to my stomach and went to the ladies room where I vomited my insides out. It looked like coffee grounds, probably from drinking so much coffee. I didn't have any breakfast before I came here so it wasn't anything I ate. It must be nerves. I heard that can make you sick or maybe I'm either coming down with a cold or have the flu.

I took a stick of gum in my mouth to get rid of that bitter taste, freshened up and went back to sit in the doctor's waiting room. The nurse finally called my name and I followed her to the doctor's office not the examining room. It wasn't to long before the doctor came in. He shook my hand and said it was what he expected but there were a few more tests he would like me to take to be sure. I told him I was willing to do anything as long as it would make me feel better again.

Dr. Madhav asked me if my appetite has improved since I'm on the pills he gave me? Not really, whatever I eat taste the same but it leaves a bitter taste in my mouth. I am forcing myself to eat like you told me to. It seems like I'm never hungry. The doctor asked me if I had any pain in my stomach or elsewhere, especially after eating? Sometimes, since my husband died, I figured it was probably nerves.

He asked me if I feel fatigued? I said yes, but I keep myself on a busy schedule which tires me out. Do you vomit after eating or even if you don't eat? It's funny you should ask me that because I just got sick to my stomach in the waiting room and went to the ladies room where I vomited dark brown like coffee grounds. I figured it was from drinking to much coffee.

Dr. Madhav said I don't want to worry you but I would like you to see an Oncologist to check you over. I'm being honest with you. It can be cancer and again it may be a peptic ulcer. But before I prescribe any medication for you I want to be sure what it is so I will know how to treat it. He handed me a card with the name of an Oncologist here in town.

I set another appointment with him for three weeks from today. As soon as I got home I dialed the Oncologist office to make an appointment to see him. The earliest I could see him was in two weeks. I set up the appointment with the receptionest but asked her to please keep me in mind if you have a cancellation. I thanked her, gave her my number and hung up the phone. I felt sick to my stomach again and made a dash to the bathroom where I vomited a very bitter, dark brown substance.

I said nothing to my children about what the doctor had suppected. They would only worry about me and Maryann would probably postpone her wedding and I didn't want anything to upset the wedding plans. I switched to tea instead of coffee to see if I would stop vomiting. I really didn't feel sick except for losing weight, no appetaite, tired all the time and now the vomiting. I had no pain nowhere.

I made a promise to myself to eat more, take my pills, and vitamins, get plenty of rest and I know I will be okay. I'm just run down that's all. I made myself lunch which was a white egg omelet with green peppers in it, two slices of low carb toast with honey on it, a orange and a cup of green tea. I did the dishes and went to soak in the tub for awhile.

I took a book and crawled into bed and started to read when I had to make a mad dash to the bathroom to vomit again. Dark brown like coffee grounds.

Maybe I can't drink tea either even though it's decaffinated, I'll just have to switch to milk and see what happens. Maybe it was nerves worried about this and the excitement of the wedding.

I rinsed my mouth to get rid of the bitter taste and turned in early. I had a very restless sleep thinking about Maryann and Mel's wedding tomorrow. I prayed to God that I won't get sick and spoil their wedding. After tossing back and forth I finally fell asleep. When I woke up the following morning I was afraid to eat anything because I didn't want to get sick in church, but if I don't eat anything I might get even sicker since I had to take my medication and I shouldn't take them on an empty stomach . So I ate a bowl of cream of wheat and a slice of toast with a glass of apple juice. I didn't want to chance it with coffee or tea. I shaved my legs and took a shower. Rubbed my whole body down with Beautiful perfumed body lotion. No sooner was I finished when I felt that bitter taste coming in my mouth. Sure enough there goes my breakfast, down the toliet.

I brushed my teeth again and rinsed my mouth with mint mouthwash to get rid of the bitterness. I put on my makeup to look alive and got dressed in my beige suit. I was craving a cigarette real bad but took a stick of gum instead. I would never go back to smoking again. Bob and I quit over twenty-five years ago. It was a bad habit to get into in the first place.

I slipped on my nylons and heels. Put on a pair of erring Bob gave me and sprayed some Beautiful perfume. Even my hair worked out perfect for me today. I looked at myself in the full lenght mirror and said not to bad for an old lady. I stuck the wedding gift in my beige purse. I dialed Maryann to see if she needed anything before I got to the church. I even got film in my camera for this happy occasion.

CHAPTER 9

▼

HAPPY TO SAD TIMES

Mel and Maryann were as happy as a lark and were floating on cloud nine. Mel surprised Maryann with a special breakfast for both of them on this once in a life-time occasion. He place a cooked egg in the center of the toast that had a heart shape. He then lined sausages to look like an arrow going through the heart.

He served orange juice in tall iced champagne glasses and had a dish of big fresh strawberries and whipped cream. They both made a toast for a long happy and loving marriage that would last forever. I told her I wish them both the best and reminded her if she didn't get off this phone she would be late for her own wedding. See you both at St. Albert The Great Church, bye, love you.

Silently I asked Bob if he was ready to see his beautiful daughter get married? Well then lets get this show on the road, ready or not here we come. On the way to the church I stopped off at the florist and picked up a pretty corsage with peach and white tea roses for Maryann and a white rose trimmed with peach for Mel's lapel.

We all seemed to arrive at the church at the same time. Mark and Amber looked sharp but no one looked as beautiful as the bride. I gave Maryann a kiss as I pinned the corsage on her suit. Then kissed Mel as I pinned his rose on his lapel. Maryann started to kid me that I always thought of everything. But I corrected her saying, see I'm not so perfect because I forgot to get flowers for Amber and Mark. What a beautiful sight to see two people so much in love. Bob would of been very proud of both of them. I can feel that Bob is here enjoying his daughter's wedding.

I asked Maryann if she had something pink and something blue, something borrowed and something new? She wore pink undies, a blue garter from Amber, a pretty crocheted hankie borrowed from her girlfriend. And as for the new well she said she has a new husband and a new life.

Father Stepek asked if Mel and Maryann were ready to get married. They both walked up to the alter were Father Stepek was standing with an alterboy. I was so afraid of getting sick and prayed very hard to help me through this cere-mony. The ceremony was short and the two happy lovebirds are now one. I know Maryann's dad was smiling down from the heaven's above.

They looked so much in love. It was like no one else was around but those two glowing. They had eyes only for each other. Here we go again, tears rolling down my cheeks but they were happy tears. I really couldn't be any happier right now except if Bob were here to walk his only daughter down the aisle and give her his blessings. I knew Bob was here in spirit, he wouldn't miss this wedding for all the money in China.

Everyone was busy kissing the newlyweds and congratulating them. I teased them that they were an old married couple of ten minutes already, see how time flies when your having fun! More pictures were being taken. They had their luggage in the car for their honeymoon so they wouldn't have to go back to the condo. There was still plenty of time to spare before leaving for the airport so we all decided to go to the restaurant to celebrate this happy occasion.

From here at the church we went to The Flame for a dinner. We asked Father to join us but he had other commitments he had to keep. We toasted the newly weds to wish them the best of everything. Good health, happiness, long marriage and Amber added and a lot of kids and we all laughed. Everyone said the meal was great but I just picked at mine. I don't know if I just wasn't hungry or if I was afraid of getting sick again. It always seemed to affect me after I've eaten something. I did eat my dessert which was a piece of white cake with fresh strawberries and whipped cream. I washed it down with some champagne. It sure tasted good. I started to feel sick to my stomach and excused myself and went to the ladies room. If I were younger I would say I was having morning sickness from being pregnant.

But I'm not pregnant and it isn't morning sickness. I stuck a stick of gum in my mouth to get rid of the taste and hoped no one could smell it on me since we were all kissing one another on this happy occasion. I put on some fresh lipstick and sprayed a little perfume on myself and left to go back to our table. Mark asked if I felt alright since I looked real pale but I told him it's the makeup.

Mel suggested they better leave for the airport or they will miss their flight. They planned to spend their honeymoon in Hawaii for three whole weeks in the sun. Of course we told them you mean three weeks in the bed which we laughed at.

I offered to drive them to the airport but Mark had everything ordered and under control. He ordered a white limousine with cooling champagne to take them to the airport. Mark wanted everything to be perfect for his only sister and his new brother-in-law. I slipped the wedding gift into Maryann's purse as I kissed her and congratulated her again.

Then I turned to Mel and welcomed him into our nutty family and said I was proud to have him for my son-in-law and kissed him too. Mark, Amber and I stood there throwing kisses and waving good-bye as the limousine pulled away and headed for the airport. I got out my hankie to wipe away the tears of happiness.

Mark and Amber asked if I would like to come to their house but I told them I'm expecting an important phone call and said why don't you both come by me?

But Amber said her relatives are watching the twins so maybe we will make it another time. We kissed good-bye and went our seperate ways.

As soon as I got home I changed into my pajamas and laid on the couch, covering myself with a blanket in the living room. I felt bad that I had to lie to my kids but I just wanted to get home and relax. I'm sure God will forgive me for telling a little white fib. I guess I must of gotten to comfortable because I fell fast asleep and didn't wake up until the following morning.

But as soon as I got up, I made a dash for the toliet. Here we go again, dark brown vomit. Maybe it was the champagne that didn't agree with me. This is ridiculous, what in the world could be wrong with me? If it is the flu, it shouldn't be lasting this long. Maybe I got some new kind of disease that no ones knows about yet. I got on the scale and I'm still losing weight. I'm 109 lbs. soaking wet.

Now I was really worried. How can I ever put on weight if I keep on vomiting? What is happening to me? Why won't anything I eat stay down in me? I wonder if Pepto Bismol would help? Maybe I ate something that didn't agree with me and I just have to get it all out of my system. I've given up coffee, tea, milk, pop, and even water, what else is there to drink?

This morning I promised myself, I will keep my food down come hell or high water. I dropped two slices of lite bread into the toaster and poured a glass of apple juice. I spread some peanut butter on the toast and started chewing it slowly, so far it is staying down.

I noticed the answering machine flashing and saw I had two calls last night. One from Mark and the other from the Oncologist. I started to dial and had to run to the bathroom to vomit. After cleaning up and rinsing my mouth I preceeded to make my phone calls. I dialed the Onocologist first and the receptionist said they had a cancellation and was wondering if I wanted to come in at 5:30 this evening? I told her yes and thanked her for calling me.

I then dialed Mark's number and hoped there was nothing wrong with the twins. Mark answered and said he was worried about me and decided to call to see if everything was alright. When you didn't answer your phone I really got worried and was going to come over but Amber stopped me and said you probably went out or was soaking in the tub to just leave a message.

I must of really been out of it not to hear the phone ring last night, not once but twice. But at least I did get a good nights sleep out of it. I finally slept like a baby without getting up even once.

Mark said I looked very pale and was so quiet yesterday that he just wanted to be sure I was alright. I told him I was fine just tired because I wasn't sleeping well. I guess the excitment of the wedding was on my mind. I was happy for Maryann but yet in a way sad since your dad wasn't alive to give her away. I missed him not being there to help us celebrate their wedding.

Mark told me he understood and changed the subject by asking me if I went to see my doctor yet? I said yes and he put me on pills to increase my appetite and pills to help me sleep. But it won't work right away, it will take a couple of days to get in my system before it works.

I promise you as soon as I feel better I will be over so much that all of your will get tired of seeing me. Mark said that will be a cold day in hell when we get tired of seeing our mom. The twins love it when you come over to play with them. And Amber and I love to spend time with you. I told him I better let him go so he can help Amber bathe the twins and give them a big kiss from grandma. Tell Amber I'll see her soon, love you, bye.

I didn't feel like reading the newspaper or the mail and really couldn't get into watching television. I went into the kitchen and changed the water in the vase of flowers from Maryann. I was thinking of how I enjoyed my honeymoon with Bob and hoped Maryann was enjoying hers too. I dusted and vacuumed and mopped the kitchen floor although it didn't need it.

I called my friend Dolores in Indiana and we chated for awhile. Pulled out the picture albums and went down memory lane again. It's funny but I never tire of looking at these pictures over and over again.

I answered a couple of letters that were lying here for weeks. Then I decided to just take it easy and relax until around 3:00 when I will have to get ready for my appointment with the Oncologist. I picked up a book and started to read but just couldn't get interested in it. Instead I ended up thinking about how time was supposed to heal the hurt of losing your spouse. But it wasn't working.

The pain in my broken heart is still there, as fresh as if it happened yesterday. Won't this feeling ever go away? Maybe missing him so much is what's making me sick. I can't get Bob out of my mind and I don't want to. We were so happy doing everything and going everywhere together.

I don't enjoy going anywhere without him. Mark has Amber and the twins. Maryann has Mel and I have my children and their spouses and the grandchildren but no spouse to love or love me. No matter how much I do or how hard I try to keep busy I just can't seem to fill that empty hole in my heart.

I wear Bob's shirts to feel close to him but it just doesn't have his body warmth. I wonder if he misses me as much as I miss him? If he is happy? If he aged or stayed as handsome as he was? Does he have a angel girlfriend up there in heaven? Is he with our parents and friends and relatives? Will we be together as he promised when I die? If only God could of given us more time to spend with each other, but there is no sense in wishful thinking.

I just have to face up to it, he is gone and never coming back. There are so many things I wish I could of said to him before he died that I will never be able to tell him but then Bob already knows how deeply in love I was with him and only him.

I always show the twins pictures of their grandpa and tell them he is in heaven with God so they won't forget about him. He sure would love playing with them. I decided to make the twins favorite cookies since I had some spare time before my appointment. I baked them a batch of double chocolate chip cookies. They end up with more chocolate on them then in them. I always felt that if a child doesn't get messy while eating, he just isn't enjoying the food.

The whole kitchen smelled great and I was tempted to eat one of them but was afraid to chance it since I was going out to see the Oncologist, I put them on a tray and covered them with foil. Washed the cookie sheets and the bowl and measuring spoons and cups. Cleaned up the mess in the kitchen and figured I would drop them off on my way to the doctors office.

I looked at the time and thought I better get going. I dropped the cookies off by Amber and she invited me in but I told her I was on my way to a friends house and was running late already. When I got to the doctor's office, it was very crowded. I signed in and found an empty chair. There were a lot of old people, some in wheelchairs. They were all friendly and joked around. Most were very thin with pale complexions. Some had very little hair and some were bald. A few women wore scarves on their heads to cover up the baldness.

I felt sorry for these people but they sure didn't want any sympathy and wanted to do things on their own.

The receptionist handed me the usual forms to fill out since I was a new patient. She then took and made copies of my drivers license and insurance cards. After filling out the forms there were more questions referring to my health. Did I have any change in bowel movements? Any sores that won't heal? Any unusual bleeding? Did I have any lumps anywhere on my body? Any coughing? Shortness of breath? Indigestion? Bone pain anywhere? Weight loss? and some of the questions were pertaining to my family. Did anyone in my family have cancer? What kind? Were they living or deceased? There were so many pages to fill out that I felt like I was writing a book.

I noticed some patients came in after I did and were already called in to see the doctor and left. Now wait a minute, that's the twelfth person they called that arrived after me. I walked over to the receptionist and asked her to check if they misplaced my name since so many people walked in after I did and have already seen the doctor. I have been waiting patiently for almost three hours.

She checked my name on the list and told me I would be called shortly. She explained that people getting chemotherapy or radiation got called sooner. I felt so foolish complaining and told her I'm sorry and went back to my seat. I never realized so many people have cancer. After waiting around eight more minutes, the nurse finally called my name.

Everyone that worked here was so pleasant to talk to. They made you feel relaxed and that they cared about you as a person no matter what color or nationality you were. You were here because you were ill and they were here to treat you and help you to feel better if they could. The nurses would joke around to make you laugh.

I followed the nurse into the doctor's examining room. She weighed me 105 lbs. Took my blood pressure 170/98 and pulse 92. The nurse wrote all this information down in a folder with my name on it. She asked why I was seeing the doctor and I replied that my doctor Gopal Madhav wanted me to be checked by an Oncologist.

Just then The doctor walked in and shook my hand as he introduced himself as Dr. Thomas Hoeltgen. He said he talked with Dr. Madhav and knew about my problem. The nurse asked me to undress so the doctor could examine me and handed me a gown to wear as the doctor slipped out of the room till I was ready.

Dr. Hoeltgen knocked on the door of the examining room to let me know he was coming in. He listened to my heart and my back. Checked around my neck, my breast and the lymphnodes. When he pressed on my stomach, I saw stars, it was very painful. He found a mass of tissue that was tender to touch. He would like to take a biopsy to complete his diagnosis. I was examined from head to toe, even inbetween my toes.

I asked him if it was cancer what where my alternatives? But Dr. Hoeltgen said lets not worry about anything until we know for sure. He suggested checking myself into Christ Hospital so he could run the tests that I would need. He asked the nurse to call the hospital to see if they had an empty room to accommodate me.

The nurse returned saying they had a room available and I could check in at Christ Hospital by 6:00 AM tomorrow morning. She handed me a prescription for medicine to get a good cleanout and to refrain from anything by mouth after 6:00 tonight. Dr. Hoeltgen said he read my chart and noticed my mother died from stomach cancer and my grand mother on my mom's side died of cancer of the Esophagas. Your grandpa on your mom's side died of cancer in the mouth and throat.

Your sister died of brain, liver, lung and bone cancer. Your dad had liver cancer but died of a heart attack and your grandpa on your dad's side died of prostrate cancer. Dr. Hoeltgen placed his arm on my shoulder and said try not to worry. I'm not going to lie to you, it could be cancer but we want to be sure so we know how to treat it.

I started to cry and he handed me a tissue. He said many of his patients have received chemotheraphy or radiation which left them in remission to lead a normal life. You may lose your hair but not your life. And your hair does grow back again. We will know more after I've seen the results of your tests. He shook my hand and said he would see me at the hospital and please don't worry and left.

CHAPTER 10

▼

A KEPT PROMISE

On the way home I stopped off at the CVS Pharmacy to pick up three bottles of Citre of Magnesia for my tests tomorrow. From there I went next door to a Subway and got myself a six inch Tuna on Honey Oak bread. They put lettuce, tomatoes, green peppers, cucumbers and black olives on it. No dressing. I was famished. This would have to last me until tomorrow after all my tests were finished.

I washed it all down with a diet, caffine free Seven Up. Boy it sure hit the spot. After I got home I was going to call Mark and tell him what the doctor said but changed my mind. There is no sense in worrying the family, anyways I don't know the problem myself until I finish the tests.

Bob is with me and will help me get through all of this with flying colors. I still feel the doctors are making a big fuss over nothing. You know how some doctors can be, they put you through every test they can think of. I'm no doctor but I still think it's a flu bug.

That would explain my sore stomach and the vomiting and with the vomiting you would have weight loss. I went into the living room and turned on the television. I have to keep myself busy so I won't think about food. It was time for me to start taking the Citre of Magnesia. Bottle number one wasn't to bad. Went back to watching television. Time for number two bottle starting to fill me up. It taste a little like a lemon lime drink except it's more gassy. The third bottle just didn't want to go down and I felt like I would explode.

I laid the mail on the kitchen table with a postcard from Maryann and Mel in Hawaii. It read Having a wonderful time. Sun is hot, water cool and scenery beautiful. Miss you. See you soon. Love The Honeymooners. I took a book and the newspaper to read at the hospital between my tests.

I sprayed a little perfume on me and locked the back door on the way out to go to the hospital. There was hardly any traffic at all. I arrived at Christ Hospital right on time 6:00. I went to admiting where everything was ready for me except my signature on the papers. A nurse took me to my room where I undressed and put on a hospital gown.

I was taken to another room and given two containers of liquid that tasted like watered down Pepto Bismol to drink. They took a test called Gastroscopy were they removed some tissue mass for the biopsy. A blood test was taken where they took two vials of my blood for testing.

A chest X-ray was taken also. They had me coming and going at the same time. I didn't care, all I really wanted to do was get all these tests over with so then maybe they will know what is wrong with me that I can't keep any food down. Dr. Hoeltgen sure is thorough and wants to solve my problems. I feel safe in his hands.

I'm begining to feel like a pin cushion with all the needles and shots for these tests. But I know it has to be done so I will just have to grin and bear it. I'll get all my tests done in one day then I can relax. My stomach keeps growling because I'm so hungry. I get a little embarassed because it's so loud but no one says anything so I guess it's normal.

Another test I received was called a Cat-Scan, with and without infusion. The doctor injected a IV into my arm which would release a saline solution into my veins as the film was rolling. They had me ly on a long table that went through a hugh donut shaped machine. It moved a little bit at a time, taking pictures of the inside of my body. A Bone-Scan was next. Then a Gallium-Scan to check my tissues.

I even received a shot of radioactive fluid and wondered if it would make me glow in the dark. I was finally finished with all the tests the doctor had ordered. I felt like I was checked inside and out, top to bottom, my organs, bones, tissues and whatever else there was to check. They wheeled me back to my room and brought in a tray with food to eat. Scrambled eggs, bacon, two slices of toast with butter or jelly. A carton of orange juice and a cup of hot water with a tea bag along side of it. Even a piece of angel food cake.

I was starved and finished everything but the tray and dishes. But it didn't stay down in me for very long. I had to make a mad dash to the bathroom where I vomited the same dark brown looking coffee grounds which left a very bitter taste in my mouth. The nurse told me not to flush it and called the doctor to check it out.

I rinsed my mouth and took a breath mint from my purse to get rid of the horrible taste. Even though I was through testing I couldn't leave until I saw Dr. Hoeltgen, so he could sign me out. So I just sat there reading the newspaper and watching television until he would come to see me. He finally walked in and said I could leave but he wanted to see me in his office tomorrow, and we can go over the results of all the tests. I said fine and left for home.

As soon as I got home, I undressed, slipped on my pajamas and crawled into bed. I was worn out. Not only tired but very weak and figured I better go to sleep before I pass out or fall down. In a way I was glad the testing was over but was afraid to find out the results.I had faith in my doctors and with all the medicines and treatments that are around I'm sure they can help me get better.

What if I had some contagious disease that I could of passed it on to the twins or anyone I came in contact with? I felt very nervous and scared to hear the truth.

After tossing back and forth I finally fell asleep and didn't wake up until the following morning. It was a gloomy day out and looked like rain.

I made the bed, then took a shower and decided to see Dr. Hoeltgen early in the morning before he got to crowded. I didn't want to eat anything since I would probably just throw it up, so I just had a glass of apple juice. I might even visit with Amber and the twins if I felt okay.

I grabbed my keys and locked the back door as I left. I made a stop at the gas station to fill up since the station was pretty empty. When I got to the parking lot it was pretty crowded and I had to drive around before I found a parking place. I took the elevator to his office and signed my name on the sheet and went to sit down.

I picked up a magazine and started to read it but not for long. The nurse called my name and I followed her not to an examining room but the doctor's office. She told me to be comfortable that the doctor would be in to talk with me shortly. All his examining rooms were filled with patients. He was a very busy doctor. I guess there are a lot of people with cancer but not that many doctors in that field.

He didn't look to happy as he pulled a chair to sit down by his desk. He had my folder in front of him and said, I'm sorry to tell you this but it's what I suspected, Cancer of the stomach. We could of done surgery to remove the affected area of your stomach, had you come to see me sooner. But your cancer has spread by metastasis into your lymp channels and your blood stream and other parts of your body.

I wish you came to me sooner then maybe chemotherapy or radiation may of helped. Right now your chances for survival aren't very good. It can be weeks or days, no one knows for sure except God. The cancer will spread rapidly invading the rest of your body with death the almost certain result. I'm so sorry but there is nothing I can do for you except to keep you on morphine to ease the pain.

You should not be alone at this time and if you want we can check you into a hospice center or if you have family that can care for you, but you won't be able to handle this by yourself. I wanted to cry but not one tear would roll down my cheeks. I wanted to scream but what good would it do me? I felt in a state of shock.

I told the doctor I wanted to die in my own home so instead of going to a hospice center I would have my family care for me. He wrote out the prescription for Morphine and said to call him anytime if I had any questions and was deeply sorry but he would keep me in his prayers. I thanked him for being truthful with me and left.

I couldn't believe this was happening to me. I had so much to live for. I don't want to be a burden to my children. I don't want them to see me in pain and feeling helpless. I want them to remember me as the happy grandma and mother that loved all of them.

I felt bad lying to the doctor, telling him my family would take care of me but my family will never know that I'm dying of cancer until I'm gone. I have gotten along fine by myself so far and will continue until death wins. How can I expect Amber to take care of me when she has her hands full with the twins, Mark is busy working and supporting his family.

And Maryann is a newlywed, finally enjoying life. No way can I burden my children. It would scare my children and the twins to see me dying in pain and all shriveled up. I want to leave them with good memories of their grandma and mom. How will my children accept my death when it was so hard for them to accept their dad's death? My children have their own lives to live and I won't interfere with their way of living.

I cried my eyes out and told Bob I might be seeing him sooner then expected. I was very depressed and my body hurt all over while my eyes burned from crying. I took a morphine tablet to help relieve some of the pain. I'm very confused, because I want to be with Bob but I want to enjoy my grandchildren and my families.

I'm not afraid to die but I don't want to suffer much. Of course I don't have a choice, it's up to God what will happen and how and when. I can pray for a happy death but can't change that my death is near. Whatever God has chosen for me I have to abide by His rules.

I want to leave something behind for my grandchildren so they will never foget their grandma. I've decided to write a short story to them. I don't know if I will be able to finish it in time but with God's help and Bob's I can try. It can tell them not to be afraid of death and that I'm still with them and will always be. That I didn't want to die right now. I enjoy playing with my grandchildren and spending time with my families. But I had no choice it was up to the good Lord and He wants me to leave my body and all my earthly possessions behind and enter His kingdom of heaven.I will never forget any of you and will be near you all in spirit. I am sad leaving you but again happy to be with my loved ones and free of pain for eternity. We all will someday be together but until then remember that I will always love you.

CHAPTER 11

ONE OF GOD'S ANGELS

I got out my typewriter and paper and started to type my short story to the twins and my family to read after I'm gone. I began.

Before God created us and the world He created the beautiful angels in heaven. Angels are spirits without bodies although they sometimes take on physical form. God gave the angels three functions to follow. To worship God, to act as His messengers between heaven and earth and to guard all humankind.

When God made us He told the angels to watch over and take care of us. Our angels go everywhere we go. When we play, go to school, work and even when we sleep. When you are afraid just talk to your guardian angel to protect and give you courage. Sometimes the angel will appear as a luminous figure as a shinning shape.

When you were a baby giggling in your sleep, it was your angel tickling you. If you feel a warmth around you, don't be afraid it's your angel sitting on your shoulder. At the time of my death, my angel will shield me from pain and fright and with their strong arms and wings, they will carry me to my new home in heaven with God and Papa Bob, your grandpa.

Remember to ask your angel for help when you need it. Sometimes God wants you to solve your own problems by yourself, so you can learn as you grow throughout your life. God doesn't want His children to get involved in frightening or evil things. Pray to your angel to help fight off evil.

When you ask your angel for help it doesn't have to be a long prayer. You can pray in any way you choose. You can use a prayer or just talk to your angel or God. And if you feel like singing then by all means sing a song. They are always near listening and waiting to help you in any way they can. Did you know that when one makes snow angels in the snow that it was to commemorate the birth of baby Jesus as the angels rejoiced?

There is even a special feast day of the guardian angels on October 2nd. This is the day to make time to thank your angel for all the help he or she has given you. Angels are not only in religious writings but in literature, music, movies, paintings, poems, television, statues, mosaics, medals and holy pictures. The angels painted in the Sistine Chapel where Michaelangelo was made famous for it, caused many people from all over the world to travel to see and admire it.

Angels are adorned with wings, halos, and harps and are always given the attributes of healing, consoling and protecting us from harm. They are loving and real and their voices not only fill the sky but fill our hearts and souls. Many people have cherubic angels on their mantles and in their flower gardens. We wear them on pins for protection. And on Valentines Day they are seen on windows for decoration for cupids. It looks like a small child with tiny wings, and a chubby belly. Some grownups even wear tattoos of angels on different parts of their bodies. Even some jewelry has angels on it like errings or necklaces. You see them in our prayer books and even on sweatshirts and tee shirts. They are everywhere.

Angels never leave us not even for a moment. These beautiful creatures of God with bright light glowing around them and wings spread out for our protection, bring us the feeling that we are not alone or afraid. Angels never fail us or are in a bad mood. God made them without imperfections. They are nothing but pure love, protection, knowledge and forgiveness.

Angels of all races attend to us humans of all ethnic backgrounds. They can communicate in many ways and usually choose to do it telepathically. Never under estimate the power and truth of what an angel can impart. They have no individuality and are never argumentative. They don't have a sense of humor but have great joy and ability to laugh. All angels have the same level of intelligence but one may have more power then another.

There are no evil angels although they do fight and dispose of evil and protect us from evil. All angels are not alike and each has different jobs to follow. Our guardian angel has to protect us from fear and phobias. The Archangels are messengers of hope and glad tidings.

The Cherubium and Seraphim angels are joyous singers in God's heavenly choir. They can produce music in it's beauty, harmony and sound that can be used for healing. These angels can also help you to remember your dreams. The Powers are healers and help with peace of mind. They surround the sick person with their wings to heal them. Of course we all know that God is the worlds greatest healer. And He proved it with the miracles He performed.

No other angel touches the dark entities but the Carrions who grab and escort them to their own holding place in God's kingdom. The Virtues angels are helpers of the charts for us mortals. They help us get the most out of life that we can for God.

The Dominions record our good deeds and actions and give us strength. These are the busiest of angels and very intelligent. They are the first angels to greet us on the otherside. The Thrones are the most highest, elevated and spiritual of all angels. They are family concious and never forget.

The Principalities are called upon to protect loved ones and everyone in danger especially children. They are guardians of the gate. They along with the Thrones are sent when there is danger or we feel mental, physical, psychic or emotional harm.

Angels have the strength to put out fires. They help us in times of distress, divorce, loss of a loved one and in physical danger. There is nothing an angel can't tackle. We each have our own angel but sometimes we need the help of other angels to aid us also. They can make our journey easier by giving us courage to face our lives or warn us so we don't take a wrong path.

Angels can't prevent all harm but they do create what we feel to be miracles here on earth and to prove to us that God is real and cares about you and me. I wonder if a pet dies if they go to heaven and if there are angel dogs? In a way it's like dogs already work for God by protecting us. Dogs keep the young ones happy as well as the old. They sit by our sides when we don't feel good and are our best friends till death.

God proved His love for us when He sent His only Son to the world so we might have life through Him. My fingers started to ache a little so I stopped typeing and decided to have a little lunch. I had a tuna sandwich with a glass of water and hoped it would stay down. Took another morphine pill because the pain was starting to come back. Made a trip to the bathroom and back to my typeing.

Do you know what happened on December twenty-fourth? A most beautiful little precious baby was born on Christmas Eve. This perfect child laid in a manger wrapped in swaddleing clothes with His mother Mary and His holy guardian Joseph in the town of Bethlehem. All the angels rejoiced and guarded the cradle of the newborn king.

The shepherds and the three kings Casper, Melchior and Balthazar honored Him with gifts of gold, frankincense and myrrh. A little drummer boy had no gift to offer to our Lord so he played his drum with love which was the greatest gift of all.

Robert and Dion did you ever wonder why Jesus who was a king wasn't born in a castle, in a golden cradle, wrapped in the best silk clothes, wearing a crown filled with gems? God could of willed it since He can do anything. Maybe it was to show us that Jesus was human just like us but was the Son of God whom we should all worship.

Wouldn't it of been nice to be present at His birth? What kind of present would you have given Him? You know Jesus could have anything but all He really wants is your faith in Him and love. He wants you to follow in His footsteps since we are all children of God. If we did, our parents would be very proud of us just like Mary, His mother was very proud of Him.

What would of happened if Mary had an abortion? Our great king, Jesus would never have been born. There wouldn't be special holidays Christmas Eve and Day to celebrate. There are so many questions that we have no answers for, like was our Lord breastfed? What did He eat as a baby? What ever happened to His umbilical cord? Was He born clean or bloody? Did He have to get baby shots? Was He colic? Did He puke like other babies do? Was He crabby when teething?

Was Jesus born with all that beautiful golden hair like we see in pictures? Was there always a halo around His head? What were His first words? Why is it we never hear anything about Jesus until the age of twelve? Did He have any playmates or a special pet like a dog?

Did He have chores to do? Did He learn to be a carpenter like His guardian Joseph? No one is alive to answer our questions. But I believe Jesus spent His time in prayer. I wonder if Jesus ever misbehaved.

We know that Joseph, Mary and Jesus went to a feast in Jeruselem. Mary thought Jesus was in the caravan but found out He did not return with them. They checked everywhere but still could not find Jesus, so they returned to Jeruselem. They found Him in the temple where teachers were asking Him questions and listening to his answers. They were amazed to see how a child of twelve could answer and understand their questions.

The next time we read about Jesus He was a gentle full grown man. Did He date or have a girlfriend? How come He never married? He loved children so why didn't He have a family of His own? Of course He did have children, we all were His children.

Jesus gave each of us a body not to be misused. A brain to think and make the right decision. A heart to feel and give love. To hate all that is evil. To honor, respect and forgive each other. He gave us eyes to see all the beauty He created around for us to enjoy.

Even though we are given the power to choose what we want out of life we should always include Jesus in our daily lives. He has given us so much and in return all we have given Him is our sins that He had died for on the cross. Have you ever thought about what it was like living at the time when Jesus was alive? Would you have been one of His close friends? Or would you have considered Him boring? He never smoked, got drunk or high on dope or picked up girls, could you be like Him?

Jesus was always helpful to others, are you? A magician can change the color of water but can he change it into the best tasting wine like Jesus did? Jesus thought us if your enemy is hungry you should feed him. If he is thirsty you should give him a drink and if he was cold you should offer him warmth. But do we do these things? If some one had no clothes would you give him something to wear?

We should learn to share our good fortune with those that need our help and there are many. We are children of God but many of us don't act like it and are very shelfish. We should open our wallets and our arms as well as our hearts to help the needy, some have no food. Some are living in cardboard boxes for shelter from the cold. Many have no medicines for their ailments. What a wonderful world this could be if we started to care about our fellow men and women.

When you swear at another, do you realize in a way you are swearing at God because God is inside everyone of us. Jesus would never use bad language towards anyone. He had respect for everyone just like we should. We are all the same no matter what color, religion, or nationality. We have to remember we are children of God.

If you see a man wearing a long dress, we consider him gay or a cross dresser. But in the days of Jesus, all men wore long shrouds. Times sure have changed, now men wear slacks or jeans. Could you ever picture Jesus wearing a pair of jeans? I don't think so. Even priests wear pants except when they are serving at mass. Then they wear a long cassock and their vestments over their pants.

Could you picture Jesus in bobby socks and gym shoes? In those days they were usually barefoot with sandals. Even soldiers boots were opened like sandals. Have you ever stopped to think how busy our Lord was when He created humans? Different sexes, races, some darker then others. Tall, short, fat, skinny, blonds, brunettes, redheads, gray and even bald. Hair was straight or curly, smooth or wirey, short or long.

Eyes of different colors, hazel, blue, green, brown and some were blessed with violet eyes. Complexions were light, fair, medium and dark. Skin texture was smooth, rough, blotchy, clear, dry, oily and flaky. People were created white, some red like the indians, black or brown like the negros, yellow like the Chinese, Philippines and the Japanese. Some were born with bulging eyes, round, slant and even some were crossed.

Eyelashes were from very short to very long and sexy. Eyebrows were short and thin to bushy. Each person was created with two eyes, two ears, two lips, upper and lower, two hands, two feet, ten fingers, ten toes, one nose with two nostrils, one head, one mouth with one tongue and no teeth but later develope thirty-two teeth. Breast were flat to overly endowed.

He furnished us with insides, a heart, liver, lungs, kidneys, veins, bones, tissues, gallbladder and muscles. Women had a vagina while men had a penis. Women could give birth but not men.

Arteries, glands, a colon, small and large intestines and everything we needed to have our bodies work properly. And to make it look attractive He had it covered with skin. Only God could create such a human being. Our God has given us so many choices to choose from in our lifetime. Do you want to marry or stay single? Do you want to have children and how many? Do you want to be a home-maker or have a career, or both?

You can be a Democrat or Republican or neither. You can decide if you want to be a Catholic, Protestant, Baptist or any other religion. Do you want to become a nun or priest? Should I drink or smoke? Each one of us has different likes and dislikes and we favor different foods and customs. Every person is an individual and has their own taste in foods, clothes, and even in friends they keep.

Have you ever noticed the noses on people's faces? All are different. Some are long, wide, pug, straight, large, turned up, flat and crooked. But they all work the same to help us breath and smell. Each enjoys different smells like in perfumes. Some like sweet smelling perfumes, some go for romantic smells, others enjoy sporty smells and there are some that prefer strong smelling perfumes and oils.

Our dress codes are different from sloppy ripped up jeans and sweats to the classy model styles. From gym shoes to eight inch heels. Our hair is worn in dif-ferent styles. Short, long, pageboy, bangs, beehives, ponytails, braids, locks, curls, waves, feathered, in a bun or straight. You can be blond one day and a redhead the next day. And if your hair is a mess you can wear a wig any style or color. Even men style their hair to their choice from shaved, crew, buzz, short to long and even in a ponytail. Our good Lord has thought of everything to please us hasn't He?

Your fingernails can be long or short and a natural color or you can cover them with a nail polish in red, pink, silver, maroon, blue, black, green, yellow or whatever color you desire. God leaves that up to you to change if you want. What a nice God, always thinking about us. How often do we think about Him? Do we even think about telling Him thank you for everything? No, we just take and keep on taking.

How could God make so many people with different colors, looks and person-alities? Only the good Lord could perform miracles like the creation of mankind. Weren't we lucky to be included in one of His miracles. From the time we were born it was up to God to plant that seed to be a girl or boy and whether it was to be one baby or two or three or more into our mother's womb. Can anyone else except Mary who is a virgin concieve a baby without sex? Only God can perform such a miracle although many girls tried to use that excuse after finding out they were pregnant and claimed they never had sex with a boy. It didn't work so don't think about trying it too.

Us women are so blessed that God gave us the opportunity to bear children. When a women delivers her baby it is so beautiful that words could never explain it and do justice. But you know in your heart that it is a miracle. To see that tiny infant that is a part of you with those tiny little fingers and toes, and that innocent look with those gorgeous eyes. Just at that very moment you know there is a God because He sent you a little angel from heaven. And to see that child growup and have children of her own and to grow old like the rest of us leading a good life for God.

Look around and see the beautiful things God created for our pleasure. The blue sky and fluffy white clouds, the warm sun, the romantic moon, rain to make the trees, flowers and lawn grow and to help the farmers grow their fruits and vegetables. He gave us four seasons, Spring, Summer which we really enjoy and Fall and Winter. Fall is nice to enjoy the trees of different shapes and colored leaves that shed their leaves but come next Spring those same trees are blooming in beauty again and again. Isn't it odd that we don't fertilize those trees but they bloom over and over again for God. He takes care of them with His rain and sun to help them grow.

Winter is a beautiful scene when the snowflakes fall and everything is covered with a white blanket of snow. That's when we make snow angels in the snow and have snowball fights, go sleding, sking or ice skating. Us elders don't appreciate shoveling the snow because sometimes the shovel gets pretty heavy. But it sure looks pretty on the branches of the trees and on the houses and lawns, it glistens.

How did we get the oceans and seas and all the fish in them? Another gift from God. When your out on the water fishing or just sailing, do you ever look around and see what God had created for you and me? And when you bait your hook with a worm or minnow or softcraw, do you wonder how it got here and why fish eat them? And when the fish aren't biting do you enjoy the beautiful scenery that's all around you?

Do you see the rabbits hopping or the deer getting a drink? The squirrels chasing one another up the trees? The racoon sitting there licking his claws? The possum and even the skunk which we run from?

We enjoy eating the fruits growing on the trees and the berries off the bushes that He created. You say He didn't create them that the farmer planted the seeds and grows everything. Stop and think! Where did the first seed or plant or man that plants them come from? Again it was the Lord. Even the air is filled with the perfumed aromas from the different flowers that grow around us in different shapes and colors and sizes.

Each flower has its own distinct aroma like a rose smells a lot different from a carnation or a gardenia. Flowers boast our moral when were feeling ill or sad. Some use the leaves from some plants or trees to cook with. Some plants and leaves and even the roots are used for medicinal purposes. Even the Dandelion which is a flower from a weed is used to make Dandelion wine. Who made all this for us if it wasn't God?

The good Lord created all the animals. Some are household pets dogs, cats, hampsters, snakes, lizards, guinea pigs, mice, pot belly pigs, and horses which many ride but are keep in a stable. Then there are animals in the Zoos that we go to see like the Tigers, Lions, Monkeys, Elephants, Apes, Zebras, Mountain Goats, Baboons, Panthers, Buffalo, Swans, Bears and etc. In the swamp areas God made the snakes and Crocodilies and Alligators and Scorpions.

There are animals that people hunt for like Bear, Deer, Rams, Wild Boars, Moose, Pheasant, Geese, Duck, Elk, and a lot more. The hunter usually has the head mounted for a show throphy, the skin or hide is tanned and used for purses, shoes or jackets or to hang for a show piece and the meat is eaten. Feathery creatures are mounted. Then put on display for everyone to see.

We enjoy the chirping and beautiful colors of the birds. The Blue Jay, Cardinal, Oriole, Hummingbirds, Wild Carnaries, Falcons, Eagles, Finches, Sparrows, Crows, Doves, Pigeons and Purple Martin which eat the mosquitoes. Other pests like the Mosquitoes are the Moths, Flies, Bees, Spiders, Centipedes and Caterpiliars which turn into beautiful butterflies. Fish and other animals feed off these insects to live. Each insect, bird and animal has a purpose on earth.

God created many different kinds of fish. Some are for eating while others are just for admiring. Like the tropical fish in our aquariums at home or the Shedd Aquarium and Sea World. Then there are the kind we fish for and enjoy eating them like the Bass, Perch, Walleye, Trout, Salmon, Crappie, Bluegill, Catfish, and more. And the good Lord gave us the biggies so we could enjoy a good fight to land them and pose for a picture with our catch or have it mounted. Some are the Musky, Northerns, Sharks, Whales, Swordfish, Marlins, Groupers and many other species.

God gave us Shrimp, Lobsters, Octopus, Snails, Oysters, Crabs and Sardines. The eyes from the Sturgeons are used to make Caviar. At night God has provided us with a romantic atmosphere with the moon glistening over the water and the stars twinkling just like they are talking to us. You can hear the owls hooting and the frogs making music with their croaking.

Isn't it nice to have such a good God that even takes care of our entertainment. He supplies us with everything the weather, the water, the bait, the fish, the sun for warmth and the beautiful scenery to enjoy all around us. And to enjoy eating the fish we caught. How can anyone say there is no God? For heavens sake look around!

God filled the oceans and seas with Dolphins, Porpoises, Sharks, Whales, Eels, Starfish, Octopus, Seals, Penguins and other water creatures. In rivers and lakes you'll find Beavers and Otters, Snakes and Muskrats that love the water. God gave us the cows which not only supply us with milk but beef as well. Pigs furnish us with pork and their skin is used for wallets, balls, purses and other things. From the sheep we get lamb and their wool is used for clothing.

Horses are used to help the farmer plow the fields. Some are in the movies and for stunts. We use them everyday for pleasure to ride horesback and in the races also in a circus. We have been provided for with poultry the Chickens, Capons, Ducks, Geese, Turkeys, Quail and Pheasant which we roast, stew, fry or make soup with. Not all are for eating some are used to lay eggs which we boil, fry, poach or use in baking and cooking.

Such a wonderful God that has given us all this and what do we give Him in return?' Heartaches! Ask yourself what can you do to thank Him for everything He has done for you? First you can begin by acting like a child of God and not a child of Satan. There is a angel sitting on your shoulder and one of Satan's evil workers sitting on your other shoulder. When a decision has to be made by you lets hope you listen to your angel since you do want to spend eternity with God and His angels in heaven and not rot in hell with the devil.

It's not easy to be good but remind yourself what Jesus went through because of our sins. We will never be perfect because only God is. But we can try our best to be like Him. To have respect for others and to show love and compassion. To help those that need our help, the needy and less fortunate.

CHAPTER 12

THE GREATEST MAN

How often do you thank God for all He has blessed you with? Do you only pray to Him when you want something? Many people have idols that they admire and would like to be like them. You will hear them say I just adore Harrison Ford and would love to be like him. Or I wish I could be like Nicole Kidman. But have you ever heard any one say I really love Jesus, I wish I could be like Him? Or I really admire the Blessed Mother Mary, I wish I could be like her. Why not?

Jesus was and is the most famous, popular and greatest man in the world and heaven but is many times forgotten, why? The movie theaters that show sex and nudity and vulgarity are crowded but not the churches that are the houses of God. There are less and less children going to church to pay their respect to God.

Children use the excuse they are to tired or don't feel well. And many parents don't care because they don't go to church themselves. But if a party is going on they wouldn't be to tired or sick to attend. What ever happened when the whole family attended mass together as a family? I hope that you Robert and Dion will attend mass with your mom and dad and say a prayer for your grandma and grandpa who love you.

We all need God in our lives every second. Where would you be if God was to tired or to sick to create you? Children will say it was their mother and father that created them but stop and think. Dad planted the cell or sperm but were did the sperm or cell come from? God has created everything even the cells and sperm to concieve babies. Without God we would have nothing.

I'm feeling a lot of pain in my stomach so I am stopping for now and will start again tomorrow, God willing. I just have to take my morphine and turn in early, I feel very tired. All I need is a good rest and I'll feel better tomorrow.

I opened my eyes and was glad to see I'm still alive. I feel so much better after a goodnights sleep and morphine. I realized why I felt so weak I forgot to eat but I know better today. I will have some cream of wheat and toast and a glass of juice then get started with my typeing. I hope I can finish my short story for the family before Mr. Death comes to call on me.

God gave us eyes to see the good He has done. And our ears to hear the word of the Lord. A mouth to receive Him in Holy Communion and not to be used with vulgarity, only praises of the Lord. A body that is clean and should stay that way and not be used wrongly. Our feet to walk the paths which were paved by the Lord to follow Him.

We all make mistakes but we should learn from our mistakes. We all need God but the poor children need Him more since there is so much temptation out there. It is all around. Children must have the love of God and fear of the devil. Children do you want to end up in the fires of hell with the devil?

The handful of children that you see in church are not even paying attention to the mass or what the priest is saying. God help our poor lost children. Many read books for relaxation. Romantic novels, crime, horror, comedy, war, fiction, pets and non fiction. But how many read the bible? They say it's to boring but it's not because you get to learn about God and Jesus, the miracles, His birth and death. Once you start reading it, you won't put it down. It's like going to mass, if you don't partake in the prayers and sing the hymns, listen to the gospel and readings and receive Holy Communion you might feel bored unless you join in.

Did you know God gave us Ten Commandments to follow? Many people don't realize that if you break one of His commandments it's a sin. You should confess to a priest for forgiveness and penance.

1. I AM THE LORD THY GOD, THOU SHALL NOT HAVE STRANGE GODS BEFORE ME.

Many adore idols like movie stars but don't even believe in God, why?

2. THOU SHALL NOT TAKE THE NAME OF THE LORD, THY GOD IN VAIN.

You can hear swearing anywhere you go by the young as well as the old.

3. REMEMBER THAT THOU SHALL KEEP HOLY THE SABBATH DAY.

One day out of seven to pay homage to God and go to church but people are to busy, tired and most just rather stay home instead.

4. HONOR THY FATHER AND THY MOTHER.

Many children have no respect for their parents, let alone honoring them. Some don't even know who their parents are while others have more then one mom or dad through divorce and remarriages.

5. THOU SHALL NOT KILL.

Adults aren't the only ones that kill, children commit murders as well as get killed. Innocent babies have been killed through abortions, left in garbage containers and found beaten till dead. Even animals that God created were tortured and killed by humans.

6. THOU SHALL NOT COMMIT ADULTRY.

This is done daily by young and old. And not only husband and wife but man with man, woman with woman and spouses with other spouses. One mate is not enough for them.

7. THOU SHALL NOT STEAL.

Most stealing starts in the home with stealing money or cigarettes from the parents and getting away with it. Some steal dope which later leads to bigger crimes like robbery or death because of it. Sometimes the stolen money is used for dope, booze, smokes, sex and gambling.

8. THOU SHALL NOT BEAR FALSE WITNESS AGAINST THY NEIGHBOR.

Be true to your neighbor and accept them for what they are not what you want them to be.

9. THOU SHALL NOT COVET THY NEIGHBORS WIFE.

Some believe in sharing or changing wives or husbands, they have no respect for others or themselves.

10. THOU SHALL NOT COVET THY NEIGHBORS GOODS.

When one does not have respect for the neighbor, then they also have no respect for the neighbors property or what belongs to them.

I hope you children will grow up obeying God's rules. Don't ever be afraid to correct someone if you hear them using God's name in vain, even if it's your mom or dad. Grandma and grandpa made mistakes with saying bad words because we were human and listened to the devil but after confession we try harder not to swear anymore. When I get mad I say San Fran Cisco California, it does help, try it.

Try to hang out with good friends and don't join gangs. There are a lot of gang wars and many innocent children and adults are killed because of it. Remember what God said "BLESSED ARE THE PEACE MAKERS, FOR THEY SHALL BE CALLED THE CHILDREN OF GOD".

We have to learn to live together in love and peace. There is so much jealousy among friends. Just as you may be jealous of what your friend has, there is someone jealous of what you have. Be thankful to God what He has blessed you with compared to what others don't have. Some have no family, friends, no food, or home to live in, no money or clothes and no one to love or care about them.

Thank God that you are alive and in good health. Many people are blind, deaf, can't speak, crippled or dying of cancer, heart problems, disease, old age and even a broken heart from lonliness.

God has given me a life to live and soon He will take that life in me away. He will send His angels to lift me up to the heavens so I can enjoy eternal life with Him and my beloved husband and all my loved ones in His kingdom. I hope you all will continue to believe in God and learn to accept whatever He has in store for all of you.

God can enlighten your mind, purify your heart and guide your every step to the right path of the Lord. When the devil tempts you to use vulgarity, say a prayer or just ask God or your angel for help. Temptation is everywhere and when you are tempted it helps to say "Our Father, who art in heaven, hallowed be Thy name, Thy kingdom come, Thy will be done on earth as it is in heaven. Give us this day our daily bread and forgive us our trespasses as we forgive those who trespass against us. And lead us not into temptation but deliver from from evil. Amen" You can even say Lord help me or just talk to Him. God is there at all times but the decision is yours whether you want to listen to God or the devil.

If people would read the Bible or prayer books they would know and believe there is a God. Look at all the miracles He performed that we read about. At the wedding at Cana in Galilee where He changed water into the best tasting wine. At Lake Genesareth where Simon was fishing without a single catch and Jesus told him to lower his nets into the deep water and Simon obeyed and caught so many fish that it tore his nets.

And what about when Jesus turned seven loaves of bread and a few fish into enough food to feed over 4,000 people that followed Him everywhere to listen to Him speak. We can't forget the blind man, who after Jesus annointed the man's eyes with smeared clay and sent him to wash in the pool of Siloam, the man was able to see for the first time in his life.

I'm sure there were many miracles that Jesus conquered that we never heard about. Remember Jesus loved everyone even His enemy. He was very forgiving. He helped those that believed in Him. If you don't believe in Jesus or God, it is never to late to start having faith in Them.

Another time Jesus was in a town called Naim, and there was a dead man being carried out. He was an only son of a widow. Jesus told the woman not to weep as He touched the stretcher and said "Young man I say to thee, arise". And the man sat up and began to speak.

In the midst of the district of Decapolis, a man who was deaf and dumb was brought to Jesus to be healed. Jesus took the man aside and touched the man's tongue and put His fingers into the man's deaf ears, looked up to heaven and said "Be thou opened". And the man's ears were opened and he could hear and his tongue loosened and he began to speak.

In Capharnaum there was a man who asked for his son who was on his death bed to be healed. Jesus said to him "Go thy way, thy son lives". And his son was healed.

Once Jesus was in a boat with His Disciples and a great storm arose and caused the boat to be covered by waves. But Jesus rebuked the wind and sea and there came a calm. The Disciples were marveled that the wind and sea obeyed Him.

Jesus was the greatest healer. He made the blind see. The lame walk. The lepers cleansed. The deaf could hear and the dead could live again. There was nothing that Jesus couldn't do.

A man whose daughter had just died asked if Jesus would lay His hands upon her and give her life. When Jesus arose to follow the man, a woman suffering from hemmorage touched Jesus's cloak and because of her faith she was well again. Jesus went into the house of the dead girl, took her by the hand and she arose and lived.

Lazarus laid dead in a tomb for four days and Jesus called out to him in a loud voice "Lazarus come out", and Lazarus arose from the dead. Jesus forgave Mary Magdalene, who was a mistress to many men and was caught in adultry and was to be stoned at the Mount of Olive. He forgave her and she changed her ways.

Jesus was a forgiving man and His heart was filled with mercy, love, kindness and patience. He thought us to hate what is evil and to do what is good. To pratice hospitality and do good things for God as well as for all that He has created. God wants us to love our enemies and pray for those that curse or mistreat us. You must learn to overcome the devil and his ways of evil.

Some of us wear medals, crosses and pins that are blessed and religious to help ward off evil which is constantly around us. We even bless ourselves with Holy Water and our houses to protect us from the devil and his works. Many carry a rosary or prayer book or bible to keep the devil and his temptations away from them.

Even Jesus was tempted by the devil himself, when he offered Jesus all the power and glory in the kingdom of the world if Jesus would only worship the devil. But Jesus refused and told the devil "You shall worship the Lord your God and Him alone shall you serve". The devil finished with every temptation he could think of without success and then departed with disguest. The angels rejoiced and came to Jesus.

Angels are always near us even though we can't see or hear them. They protect us and guide us the right way. Angels even watch over us when we sleep. But it is your choice to listen to your angel or the devil and his evil works. Your angel will never give up on you.

There is a prayer especially for our guardian angels. "Angel of God, my guardian dear, To whom His love commits me here, Ever this day be at my side, To light and guard, to rule and guide. Amen." You must remember that God created us beautiful creatures so we can join Him in paradise when our time on earth expires and not to burn in the fires of hell with the devil. But it is our decision to choose.

We should all walk in the footsteps of the Lord since we are His children. At the end of the world, the angels will go out and seperate the wicked from among the just, and will cast them into the furnace of fire, where there will be the weeping and gnashing of teeth. Let us hope we are among the just and end in heaven.

Jesus and His Father God love us, so do not let anyone lead you astray or to have you become a partaker of the devil or his works. Remember blessed are those who hear the word of God and keep it.

It's ashame that today there are so many children as well as adults that don't believe in God or pratice any religion. Just like at Christmas time you will hear children cry out to see Santa Claus but have you ever heard a child say Mommy I want to go see Jesus? If it wasn't for Christ being born there would be no Christmas. See the spelling of Christmas it has C H R I S T name in it. We don't call it Santamas. You will see decorations of Santa Claus, Mrs Claus, Elfs, the Grinch, Soldiers, Bears, Candy Canes and many more. But how many Nativity scenes do you see? And that's what Christmas is all about. At least the churches still reconize the true spirit of Christmas. Christmas and Easter are about the only two times that you'll find the churches full of people and most go to Communion. I'll bet our Lord is smiling on those two days.

We complain about everything but not our Lord even when He had reason too. Look at how many people spat on Him or struck Him with palms when He walked by. When they placed those piercing thorns that were made into a crown on His head. Can you feel what agonizing pain our Lord was in? But not a whimper from Him. And with all that pain He still had to carry that heavy cross and never once did He cry out.

You know how it hurts when you stick yourself with a needle or pin. But how much do you think it hurt our Lord when they drove those nails into His hands and feet? His holy blood dripping from everywhere. If you had to change places with Jesus, do you think you could of stood the pain without passing out?

Even though Jesus suffered with pain from His head, hands and feet they still pierced His side and gave Him more pain to endure. Jesus didn't deserve any of this but He did it to forgive us our sins. Would you give up your life for the mistakes of others? You would probably yell and scream and say don't take me! Take someone else!

How can you not love or have faith in a great man that gave up His life for you? Could you have risen from the dead like our Lord did? Jesus never hated anyone for what they did to Him. He only died on the cross and accepted what God the Father had in store for Him. Could you be so forgiving as our Lord? Are you willing to accept what God has in store for you?

God is love and loves you as well as me and teaches us to love one another. God is in us all so if someone says they hate you, it's the same as saying they hate God. All of us must believe in our Lord and we will be saved but those that don't have the faith will be condemned. What more proof do you need to believe there is a God?

CHAPTER 13

▼

THE END IS NEAR

God realizes we are not perfect but He would like us not to be liars or hypocrites. When you lie to someone, you are lying, to God. The devil is like a hungry lion waiting to devour you. You have to resist him. You must be strong and steadfast in your faith in God so you can enjoy eternal glory with God in heaven.

Jesus is our shepherd and we are His lost sheep. He laid down His life for His sheep and other sheep that are not of His fold. But after hearing His voice there shall be one fold and one shepherd. Jesus rejoices when one sheep repents, more then if the rest of the herd had no need of repentance.

We who love God and life and see good days should refrain our tongues from evil and our lips to speak only the truth. We must turn away from evil and do good for the eyes of the Lord are upon us and His ears listens to our prayers and grants us the favors that we pray for. He never turns away and is always there to console us when it's needed. He is your best friend.

Your family, relatives, friends and even your pets will leave you but our Lord is here to stay forever on earth and in heaven. You can always trust Him since He only speaks the truth. There are times things happen that we don't like but He has a good reason for it and we just have to accept it even when it isn't pleasant for us. God works in mysterious ways.

He knows what is good for us even if we don't. We must put our lives into His hands and just keep our faith in Him. Do you really think that a man that has gone through so much pain dying on the cross for us would try to harm us? He loves us much to much to hurt us in any way and wants to spend eternal life with us.

I find myself getting weaker as the days go bye. I have to call Amber and talk to the twins so they won't suspect I'm dying. I dialed her number and Amber answered. I spoke softly and slowly so I wouldn't make any mistakes. I talked with the twins for a short while and back to Amber. I explained I would come over to visit but I have a cold and don't want the twins to catch it from me.

She asked what I have been doing and I told her just lying around and taking it easy. Amber was going to drop over with the twins but I talked her out of it saying to make it another time when I don't have a cold. She hung up saying to take care of my cold and feel better soon. I felt horrible lying to her but I want them all to have good memories of me not what I look like now.

When they read what I wrote I'm sure they will understand why I did things this way. After all there is nothing anyone can do to change things. I'm dying and that is it. After having a sandwich and juice which I still threw it all up I went back to typeing my story. It really felt stupid to eat if I keep throwing it up but if I don't eat I probably wouldn't have any strength at all.

THE END IS NEAR   121

I hope God will give me enough strength to finish what I want to do. In my story I asked the twins, if you were invited to a birthday party for Jesus, what kind of present would you give Him? He can have anything He wants but from you all Jesus would want is your faith in Him and your love.

None of us know when or how we will die but we must be free of sin in order for your soul to join God in heaven. You can die of cancer like me or have a heart attack. Be in a bad accident, or burned in a fire. You can drown, get killed in a war, choke on food even die during surgery or from a disease. Only God knows. Our angels work for God and follow His orders to come for us when it is time.

Isn't it odd that us homeowners who have beautiful, weedless, green lawns had to work hard to get it to look that good. Planting grass seed or laying sod, watering, fertilizing, mowing, areating, weeding and raking. Yet God created trees, flowers, bushes, shrubs and wild grass that are never fertilized and still they bloom beautifully with God's rain and the Sun and His love.

He even takes care of the beautiful birds in the sky and in return they rejoice with their melodies of love to Him. Many of the animals feed off the trees or berries on shrubs and even other insects or animals to survive. All supplied by the one and only Lord.

Miracles take place everyday when a baby is conceived in a mother's womb. The seed is planted by God and grows to be a child of God's. If anyone experienced the birth of a newborn, they would agree it is a miracle to see this new life come into the world so beautiful and innocent.

To enjoy the pleasure of holding this precious gift from God. Those tiny fingers wrap around your finger and hold on to your love. The magic of that little heart beating, the tiny lungs and turned up nose to breath, the fight in that little body to go on living. It is a little package of love, all done by the works of the good Lord and the help of both mates who will protect this precious baby with all their heart.

Women are blessed by God that they can have the opportunity to have children although some can't but they still have the pleasure of raising them when they adopt. Even though a man cannot concieve or deliver a baby that child is part of him too. And he can enjoy being a good father to his son or daughter. That baby may have it's dad's eyes or nose or color of his hair. Sometimes the baby won't look like either parent until they get older or they might resemble a grandparent. The looks don't really matter, what counts is that the baby is healthy and loved by both parents not just one.

God made man to love one woman not two. For he will hate one and love the other or he will stand by one and despise the other. The man or woman only deceives himself or herself. When a man or woman is tempted, they should put on a suit of God's armor so that they can stand up against the devil and his ways. Bind your loins with truth. Wear your breast plate of justice, conseal your feet with the readiness of peace, put on your helmet of salvation and use the sword of the spirit that is the word of God.

We, the people have to change for the better and make it a better world to live in. We should be concerned parents and take our children to church as a God loving family would. So our children can learn how to honor God, fear the devil and have respect for all mankind. That no one will have a garbage mouth using God's name in vain, only speak His name in praise. Even the young ones swear since they hear it in their own homes from their parents and brothers and sisters or friends. Children must gain respect for their parents.

If you have respect for your parents and them for you, it will be easy to have respect for your neighbors and their property too. Just as we have the fear of hell and the devil, we should have the fear of disobeying our parents as well as the love and trust for them. When you love someone you don't hurt them by not listening to them. You may not like what they tell you but they know what is good for you even if you don't agree with them.

You may get away with telling a few lies now and then to your parents or friends but what happens when you have to face the Lord? Then you won't be able to lie your way out because it is written in the charts. When you were baptized your soul was beautiful and pure. But as you get older your soul becomes disfigured and dirtied with sins.

Only confession and the good Lord can restore your soul to it's former beauty. It's very easy to sin with all the temptation of dope, alcbhol, sex, nudity, vulgarity, stealing, murder and even missing mass. And of course you want to be like everyone else in the crowd so you join in with the rest of the evil dwellers.

Don't forget that drinking or pot leads to other things like sex and unwanted babies or self destruction of ones body. It ends up to be one sin after another. Just think if you had to die on the cross with a crown of thorns placed on your head and nails in your feet and hands because of your sins, would you still sin?

I told you before it isn't easy being good and sometimes you won't even have any friends because they will consider you dull but it is very rewarding in the end. Don't be a follower unless your following in God's footsteps, otherwise be a leader and help those evil doers to become children of god.

Death can be beautiful, I don't mean the way some die but afterwards when the Carrions come to carry your soul to a holding place in God's kingdom. The evil dwellers suffer because their soul ends in hell with the devil, who they lis-

THE END IS NEAR   123

tened to instead of their angel. Our Lord has saved some of those souls when they showed remorse and faith in God and asked Him for forgiveness of their sins. Many don't know how to accept the death of a loved one. Each has it's own way to relieve the hurt.

My cancer is to far gone and there is no cure to help this unbearable pain. It will be a blessing when God sends His angels to take me into His kingdom of heaven where I will be painless and with my loved ones. I am greatful that God will choose me to be one of the lucky ones to be living for eternity with Him and my loved ones especially Robert. Think of it not as the ending of my life but the begining of a new life.

I hope you all can forgive me and understand why I didn't want anyone close to me while I was dying. You would just try to hold onto me and I wanted to leave in peace and end my suffering and join God. Death cannot be so bad, after all many people that died were smiling. Maybe it was because they saw the light and all the beauty that they will be surrounded by.

I never found happiness since your father died and missed him so much. Maybe I should have married again to help fill that empty feeling in my heart. Even though I had you my children and my grand children, it wasn't the same as having your spouse with you. I wish that God would have taken me instead of your dad.

So many questions that went unanswered maybe now God will answer them for me. Like was it wrong for me to love my husband so much? Was I being punished for something? Why did God choose to take Robert when there are so many people around? Was God testing me?

If I had married again, my new husband could never replace my beloved but it might of helped fill the loneliness. Even though I could of fallen in love again, Robert would always have a special place in my heart. God wants us to go on living until your time is over in this world. No one can understand the feeling a spouse goes through unless they too have lost their spouse.

Everyone has to learn to accept death as well as life. God takes not only the old but children and even babies, some through stillborn at birth. Don't pray for me when I'm gone but for you so that God can give you the strength to go on without me. Just as you have learned to accept your father's death, you now will have to accept mine. And be happy for me not sad. Think of me as free of pain, living in peace.

Don't fret because we will be together again when God wills it. I had to stop again the pain is getting worst and comes more frequent. The morphine doesn't seem to help anymore but I grin and bear it just thinking about the pain our Lord suffered for me on the cross. I'm experiencing nothing compared to what He had to suffer. I fell asleep on the couch but had a restless sleep.

When I woke up I took some more morphine and went back to type some more. At least you will have your mates to help heal the hurt. I had many friends when dad was alive. And a lot of them at the wake and funeral but after that day it seemed you are forgotten. Women are afraid you might go after their husbands, now that your single again.

All I ever wanted was someone to talk to and console me. But it seems everyone is to busy. I didn't want to become a jealous or bitter person I just wanted to be a friend. That's when I learned my only true friend was God. He would listen to me and help heal my pain from losing my Robert. And now children I want you to talk to God or your angel.

Don't hold the tears back, have a good cry and get on with your life. Remember the precious times we shared together and the happiness we had. I may be leaving you but I will always be with you even though you won't see or hear me. You will be surrounded by my love. Who knows maybe I will be chosen to be one of your angels watching over you. I hope you will always remember your grandma because she will never forget any of you.

CHAPTER 14

TOGETHER AGAIN

Thank you God, for helping me to finish my short story to leave to my children, so they will be able to understand why I did things this way so they wouldn't have to see me suffering. I hope now that you will find it in your heart to help me to finish my manuscript before I leave this world to enter your kingdom of heaven. I know you will because I have faith in you, oh, my God.

God hasn't forgotten anything to please us. We can even change the color of our eyes with contacts. We can lose weight to get skinny or gain weight to get hefty. When you lose your teeth, you can get a pair of false teeth, that help you to chew. If you lost a limb, the doctor can fit you with a prosthesis, which is an artificial leg or arm that can work as a real one.

Even though each one of us was created the same we have different likes and dislikes in people, music, food, customs, dress, movies and even where we live. Some live in houses or condos and some rent an apartment. And when we get to old and can't handle things we can live in a retirement or a nursing home. Just as He created all humans, God created many different species and breeds of animals for us to enjoy as a pet or just to admire not to destroy.

Look at all the different languages that are spoken and yet we can communicate with each other. Even the ones that can't speak learn to talk through hand signals or lip reading. The blind can read with Braille. Animals can't speak in words but bark and do understand when we talk to them. What a wonderful God we have who cares about us all.

Some snakes, scorpions and black widow spiders can kill us with their venom but again their venom can cure us in certain cases. God created the tiniest flea to the largest dinosaur. Some animals we enjoy as our pets while others are in zoos and jungles. Some we use for food and clothing and some are even used for testing our new medicines.

What a great God always thinking about His people and not Himself. Each animal has a purpose on this world and sometimes is used for food for another animal to survive. We also were put on this world for a purpose and when we are through, God will come to take us. You can see how forgiving God is to give us so much after what our sins did to Him.

How anyone can say there is no God is unbelievable. Who created the earth we live in? The planets? The sky and clouds even the sun and the moon which we see in different shapes? Who filled up the seas and oceans with water and put fish in them? Who put the stars in the sky and why do they twinkle? Who made the rain, snow, sleet, storms, floods, earthquakes, tornadoes and avalanches?

How can a human cell develope into a baby and grow into an adult? How can grass, trees and wild flowers grow without fertilizer and no one planting them?

TOGETHER AGAIN   127

Who gave us the four seasons, winter, spring, summer and fall? Only God can change the daylight into the darkness of the night.

We all take to many things for granted and we can lose everything in a second. The loved ones that have passed on are lucky because we here on earth live in hell with crime, war, jealousy, hatred, murders, bitterness and robberies. When was the last time you thanked Jesus or your angel for protecting you from all this? And they don't get paid for watching over you but do it because God wants them to protect us since He loves His flock.

Our angels are always near us to help us lead a good life but we have to do our share too. They help us not to be afraid of dying. Death isn't the end but instead a new begining in a peaceful world filled with love and your loved ones.

I know my time is near to depart from this world and I have to figure out how to have my death taken care of without upsetting my family. I must get someone I can count on to get my body over to the undertake as soon as I have passed on since I wouldn't want to be found months later I've gone. I have everything else taken care of for my burial and my plot is paid for. I left all the instructions down of how I want my funeral handled.

The chapel, church, cemetery, songs I want played at the mass, the restaurant for the luncheon afterwards. I even have my obituary column typed. It was all in a envelope with money to pay for the luncheon and open bar in case anyone needed a drink. The only thing that has to be done is to get my body delivered to the undertaker so I could be waked at the funeral home.

I need someone I can trust and would not tell my family until I'm gone. I opened my address book and at the very begining in the A's was my best friend Dolores Anderson. I know I can count on her. We have been through thick and thin for many years.

I dialed her number and she answered after the first ring. I then explained everything to her and she said she was sorry to hear the news about my health but had agreed to call me everyday. In case I didn't answer she would try once more and if I still didn't answer, she would come over to check if it was all over. I told her I had a spare key hidden under a false rock by the door. It might sound morbid to talk about my death this way but it had to be done and by someone dependable.

I told Dolores she would find the envelopes on my kitchen counter by the telephone. There was Mark and Ambers phone number too. As for Maryann and Mel, well they were on their honeymoon but there was a number to call in case of emergency. And the number for the funeral home.

I hated to cut Dolores short but the pain was unbearable and I was to weak to continue our conversation or even hold the phone. The Morphine isn't doing anything for me now, it's the same as if I took candy. I hung up and went to the kitchen counter and checked that everything was okay. All the bills were paid up to date. The envelope was marked important information which held my funeral plans.

There was another envelope marked IN CASE OF DEATH OPEN, which contained my will and birth certificate and important papers the undertaker would need. I added that I wanted the pallbearers to wear a rose in their lapel that they would ly on my coffin with their white gloves at the burial site.

The Social Security would have to be notified to stop payments to me and my insurance company. My family never suspected I was in deep pain or dying since I hid it well. If they saw me now it would scare them. I really believe its better that they have good memories about the way I looked.

I hope they will be able to cope with my death and that they can find it in their hearts to forgive me for not telling them I was dying. I will miss all of them especially my grandchildren. I have led a good life and now am ready to leave it all behind when God calls me. I walked slowly to my empty bed and felt I better get in before I fall down. I asked myself, how much longer can I go on?

I crawled into the bed and covered myself up to my neck. As I laid there so many happy memories of the past flashed before my eyes. My children were all raised well with the belief of God so I know He will help them cope during the time they will be grief stricken over my departure from this world.

I snuggled next to Bob's pillow wrapped with his robe. I held onto it tightly and fell fast asleep. I was dreaming that I was standing in a large field surrounded by beautiful flowers in many different gorgeous colors and fragrants. I could hear flapping of wings like birds only bigger. As the sound drew closer, I noticed many angels with different colored wings coming down towards me from the magnificent, blue sky.

They all seemed to circle around me. Some were singing with such angelic voices that it was heavenly to listen to. Two of the angels took hold of my hands and started to guide me towards a bright, luminous light, shinning from the heavens above. I could see in a distance a figure of a man with a dog. Both were running towards me and there were many people behind them.

The man had his hands outstretched as if to wrap them around me in an embrace. As the figures grew closer I could make out a human form. As it got much closer I could see it was Bob, my beloved husband with our dog Queenie. The people behind looked like my mom and dad and all my deceased relatives.

TOGETHER AGAIN   129

Soon we reached each other and embraced in each others arms and Bob kissed me gently on my lips and whispered. Darling don't be afraid, I told you we will always be together. Bob ever so gently took my hand in his and we walked into this bright light that was almost blinding but beautiful.

Bob and I were skipping as we swung our hands and Queenie was jumping for joy at our sides while our faces were full of happiness and contentment. So many people were coming towards me to greet me. I saw grandma and grandpa, my mom and dad, Bob's mom and dad, our deceased aunts and uncles, friends and neighbors and even my childhood pets.

I was over joyed seeing everyone again and not one of them aged, Even Bob and Queenie looked the same as on earth. This must be what heaven is like since everything is so perfect and beautiful. The men wore pastel blue shrouds while the women wore pastel pink. I could see a man sitting in a throne in a white shroud with a bright halo around His head and bright lights surrounding Him with angels every where.

He must be God. I was very anxious to meet with Him and had a million questions to ask Him. Only He could give me answers. There were many other people and children standing in a long long line to see Him. I guess I will just have to wait my turn. What a beautiful place this is to spend eternity. Everyone is smiling and no one is in pain.

As I turned around and glanced down toward earth, I could still see my shrunken body lying very still in the bed where I was sleeping. There was this very peaceful smile on my face. All of a sudden I became aware that this was not a dream at all but it was really happening. I died and God sent His angels to come and carry me to His kingdom of heaven.

I am now in God's hands in the house of the Lord called heaven. To share eternity with Him and my husband and all my loved ones. I'm just glad my soul was pure otherwise I would rot in the fires of hell.

This is were I belong with my husband and loved ones and someday my children and grandchildren will be here to join us. Bob did not let me down, he kept his promise to me just like he said he would.

WE WILL ALWAYS BE TOGETHER. The end or is it? It might just be the begining of a new life for the both of us to enjoy for eternity.

THE END
M.S.M.

WE WILL ALWAYS BE TOGETHER

We will always be together and never apart,
I promise you from the bottom of my heart.
Although we shared happiness from day to day,
Death parted us as we went our seperate way.
I live each day with you on my mind,
Remembering you were thoughtful, loving and kind.
I miss our talks while walking hand in hand,
Soon God will call me to His promised land.
Time doesn't heal, my heart aches with pain,
I want to be with you in heaven again.
Queenie is missed and my beloved family,
God's angels will guide me to you for all eternity.
In life and in death no matter what is the weather,
As you promised, We will always be together

By Margaret Seiders-Metz

The Author
Margaret Seiders-Metz

Margaret and her husband Bob live in Burbank Illinois with their two dogs Lady and Rainy. She is the mother of four, the late Maryann, Marcia Schmitt, Michael Seiders, and Marie Martinez. A grandmother of seven, Steve, Dan and Kevin Schmitt, Chrissy and Brian Seiders and Nick and Marissa Martinez. She loves working in her flower and veggie gardens or relaxing on their pontoon in Indiana. Margaret has already published a book "The Dog Nobody Wanted" and is working on "My Cherished Memories".

978-0-595-37948-4
0-595-37948-6

CPSIA information can be obtained
at www.ICGtesting.com
Printed in the USA
FFOW04n1544101216
30258FF